CASE LOAD–MAXIMUM

CASE LOAD-MAXIMUM

by E. RICHARD JOHNSON

1817

HARPER & ROW, PUBLISHERS

NEW YORK, EVANSTON, SAN FRANCISCO, LONDON

A JOAN KAHN–HARPER NOVEL OF SUSPENSE

FIRST EDITION

STANDARD BOOK NUMBER: 06-012213-7

LIBRARY OF CONGRESS CATALOG CARD NUMBER: 72-160659

1

It was the lame end of the graveyard shift, the hour in the morning when the city sleeps while the night edges the day's heat from the silent buildings.

It had been a hot summer. It was now September, though the heat showed no sign of weakening its grip on the city. Everybody knew that September was the cooling-off month. The month of cool nights and warm days, with a brisk tang of frost during the mornings, the month with that hazy look of smoke in the air during the afternoons. Everybody knew that.

Someone hadn't got the word.

It was September 15, and as hot during the day as it had been on July 15. It was the kind of heat that seemed to follow you around, hanging close and damp, and there was nothing that could be done about it.

Leo Stanley, the patrolman on Sunset Avenue, had reported for duty at 5 P.M. with the rest of the graveyard shift. He would go off duty at 5 A.M. No matter how thankful Stanley sometimes felt about the brief, cool hours of early morning, there was no getting around the fact that he still had one more hour of sidewalk pounding to be done before he went off duty.

And his feet hurt. You could tell Stanley how lucky he was to escape the heat, and about all the short-tempered citizens who went with it, and he would tell you to stick it in your ear.

1

Those few cool early hours weren't all fun and games. They had their disadvantages. Like that damn mist. Just as soon as the cool air and the warm water in the lake over in the park got together, the mist would come creeping into the city like massed ghosts.

By four o'clock in the morning, the mist was hanging over the streets and haunting the alleys as far up as Sunset Avenue. So you could tell Stanley about those nice cool hours, all right, but it wouldn't make him thankful for them.

About all Stanley could say for the morning hours was that they were generally quiet. He had been a patrolman for six months, but he still thought the quiet, coupled with the mist, made it a spooky time to be pounding a beat, whether you were cool or not.

He looked at his watch as he walked. The owner of the café at the end of his beat would be on the job in about forty-five minutes, and Stanley would go around to the kitchen door and get a cup of coffee to help him greet the new day with a smile.

There was no one on the street as far up as he could see. If he checked the alley as he went down, and came back out for a look at the street every two blocks or so, he would cover both parts of his beat at the same time, and he would have fifteen minutes of extra time when he reached the café.

He reached the corner. Well, he really couldn't cover the street part of his beat like that. But it was nice and quiet on the street. The alley now, that was where any breaking and entering would be done, if anyone was going to do it.

He clicked on his flashlight and turned into the alley. Fifteen minutes were a lot of minutes when you were in the

2

eleventh hour of a long dozen. He would have enjoyed every one of them if he had made it.

The mist was thicker in the alley, hanging in belt-high wreaths, like fingers of dirty cotton. His light played over the piles of rubbish, and fastened itself briefly to the closed doors and windows as he walked. For a while, the only sounds were the muffled slap of his shoes.

Then he heard the cat.

The yowling came from the mist and dark ahead of him. Stanley stopped and listened. He did not like cats. He was one of those people who never had seen anything sweet or cuddly about a cat. They were too sneaky and silent for him.

He could never think about a cat without thinking about dead bodies. He blamed his father for that, because his father had once told him a story about a cat slipping into an open casket and later scaring the pants off everyone at the wake with its yowling to be let out.

He transferred his flashlight to his left hand and unsnapped the leather strap that held his service revolver in its holster. There was nothing moving in the alley but the mist. He pointed the torch ahead and went warily toward the sounds.

A collection of garbage cans stood in scattered ranks along the back door of a bar, with just their heaped tops rising above the mist. The cans reminded Stanley of tombstones. And on the top of one of the cans the beam of his flash spotlighted a cat.

The cat stared calmly at Stanley and yowled.

Feeling somewhat foolish about the unsnapped holster, and the way that the hair on the back of his neck was behaving, Stanley walked nearer.

3

All right, all right, he told himself. There isn't a thing wrong with that cat. He's a nice cat, and if I just go up there and pet him, he'll probably purr or something.

The cat watched him balefully as he approached.

"Nice kitty," Stanley said, and jerked spasmodically as the cat spit at him and jumped to the alley's concrete floor. He followed the cat with his light, and felt a cold shock creep through him as the beam illuminated a girl's body.

She lay on her back among the overflowing garbage. She seemed to be stretching in sleep, but under her head, on the scattered pages of yesterday's newspapers, and reaching out past them, was a dark pool of blood.

She might once have been described as a pretty girl. Only now her face was coldly blank in death. She was wearing an opened white blouse, and a rose-red skirt, and shoes that were little more than straps, and her skirt had been pulled down so its belt line was just below her knees. It was bunched in a red rumple that covered just her shins. There was no sign of under-clothes.

Whatever Stanley's other feelings were at finding a corpse, he felt a sudden embarrassment about the girl's exposed naked-ness as the initial shock wore off. There were certain things that he felt should accompany death, such as the dignity of being covered.

He turned the harsh light of his flash away from the body and started walking toward the street and a telephone, playing his light over the shadowed rubbish, and thinking about that goddamn cat. He was no longer bored, or considering his aching feet.

There was nothing like a body to start the day with.

4

2

A fair share of lousy people live in every city.

Mose Hamilton was undoubtedly the lousiest and meanest human being on the detective squad working out of the East Bagley Street police station. In all probability, he was the lousiest human being on the city's entire detective force. There was nothing Hamilton liked better than locking some punk up in the slammer. He would have liked it even more if he had been permitted to weld the door shut after he had locked it. Their guilt or innocence never entered into his thoughts as he locked up punks. A punk was always guilty of something, and if he didn't want to be locked up, he should stop being a punk; or better yet, a punk should go someplace where Hamilton's attention would not be focused on him during an investigation.

Hamilton considered any suspect in any case as a punk. Also, he had a definite leaning toward the Gestapo technique of questioning suspects when he considered the answers that he was getting were untrue. About the only way suspects could gain Hamilton's approval would be by carrying a signed confession in their pocket, just giving him the opportunity to fill in such minor facts as time, place, and crime committed.

It was difficult to understand then how he could be a good cop while he went on being a lousy human being. You can be

5

a lousy human being and be a cop, just like you can be a lousy human being and be a plumber.

Discouragement, exhaustion, and dull routine can make some people lousy human beings. And when you add things like too much crime and too few policemen, coupled with large doses of liars, thieves, and butchers in an environment where human decency seems to be in a state of suspension—well, that might do it too. And then you top these things off with years full of gun battles in dark alleys, and bloody street fights where the blood and broken bones are often as not your own.

All that might even give you the impression that it doesn't pay to be a nice guy, because nice guys finish last, with split heads. You might get paranoid about the whole business and decide to be a lousy human being, just to be on the safe side. If you did, you might wind up not liking people of any kind; punks or not.

Hamilton no longer cared if he became the scourge of the underworld, as he'd intended to when he joined the force nineteen years before. He would now play it for existence. He was full of suspicion and resentment and fallen ideals. He had a feeling of perpetual exhaustion when he worked. But he would survive; he would take any bitter pill that life could toss his way and shrug it off. He was no longer impressed with life, himself, or his fellowman.

He began his day as usual with a silent four-thirty breakfast in the all-night diner near his apartment. The graveyard shift was considered off duty at 5 A.M., and it was the practice of the relieving detectives to turn up at the station house between four thirty and five, in order to get any items of interest that the homeward-bound detectives might care to pass on but did not consider important enough to type into a report.

Sometimes it is best not to be such an eager beaver. There were days that just started out wrong and it didn't pay to make them any longer than you had to.

He had thought at breakfast that it was going to be one of those days. He knew it was going to be hot. It had all the signs for that; there wasn't a hint of a breeze or a sign of a cloud in the lightening sky. And the sky was already beginning to take on that brassy color in the east. Besides all that, he had listened to the weather report on his car radio when he drove to the station house. It was going to be a clear, cloudless day, with no wind. It was going to be a hot son-of-a-bitch again.

The station house was the hottest place in the city too, if you could believe the bulls who worked out of it. It was a four-story granite-block structure, built like a fort, that seemed to hold the heat like an oven. It was no place to work in. The day shift would open the windows hopefully and prop open the double doors facing the street in anticipation of some spare breeze that might find its way over from the park. But the only thing that seemed to find its way into the station was the reek of gasoline fumes and punks.

Hamilton hated the heat almost as much as he hated punks. The past weeks had merged into an exhausting routine of boredom and heat, where all he seemed to be doing was answering endless squeals. Or he was at his desk, typing reports, which made him think it would be nice if he could team up with one of the other four detectives on the shift, then *he* could type endless reports and Hamilton could sit still and sweat in comfort by virtue of his detective-first-grade rank.

7

Only there was a marked reluctance of any of the other four detectives to team with him.

So screw them, he thought, in his usual humor that morning. He liked working alone. He didn't have to worry about getting reported for blackjacking some punk by any candy-ass excuse for a cop.

He had reached the station at his usual time. It had taken him five minutes to read the logbook on the desk sergeant's bench near the door and to learn that it had been a reasonably quiet night. He also had learned that the on-duty detectives were out on a prowler call. And with the exception of Lieutenant Kinsmiller, who was in his office, the relieving shift had taken advantage of the time to head for the corner drugstore for coffee. Hamilton had headed for his desk with the intention of getting some of yesterday's reports typed while it was still relatively cool and he could sit at his desk without his shorts creeping into a ball at his crotch. He had tortured himself for some minutes with the thought of just how hot it would be in a few hours, before he fed a limp form into the typewriter.

Lieutenant Joseph Kinsmiller heard the typing start in the squad room. He knew, without going to the door and looking out, that the typist was Mose Hamilton. There are very few minutes during a cop's day in which silence prevails over his place of work. Silence is golden; it is something to be appreciated and cherished, and used to its last golden second. And only Hamilton would screw that up. Hamilton would, in fact, screw up a wet dream if Kinsmiller had not long ago passed the age where he had them.

Kinsmiller had tried to understand it. He realized that Hamilton was an old cop, and that it was difficult to adjust to

8

changing times when you were still dealing with people who played by the same old dirty rules. Kinsmiller also agreed that there were occasions when a bit of blackjack psychology was needed to make some hophead come down to the station house for a chat. Only Hamilton's arrests had a habit of being brought to the station with more than what Kinsmiller could consider a normal amount of bruises. Still, he could not condemn a man for that; he needed a few tough cops on the force if it were for no more than the deterrent effect they had on the repeat offenders who lived around the station, which was not located in the Nob Hill section of the city by any stretch of the imagination.

But Hamilton's effect didn't stop there, and Kinsmiller was finding it increasingly hard to justify him as a cop when he treated all the men at the station house as though their main interest in life was to make Detective First Grade Hamilton's life difficult. It was simply hard to understand why the man insisted on making everyone dislike him. The station house, which Kinsmiller had skippered for seven years now, was like one big family. Patrolmen and detectives alike worked together with a minimum of sparks between personalities, which was an accomplishment in itself. They did this with one exception, and even in that one exception the others agreed.

The exception, of course, was Hamilton. The others wholeheartedly concurred that while he might be a good cop, with a lot of solved cases behind him, he was also the most antisocial, antagonistic son-of-a-bitch in the city. And if Kinsmiller wanted any of them to team with him, he had better get the transfer papers out.

Kinsmiller did not enjoy the atmosphere that Hamilton created around the station house. He had considered asking

9

the brass to transfer him out to some other precinct, where the sparks he caused would be someone else's headache. With this in mind, he had got Hamilton's department file to determine if the man was qualified for a desk job.

After he had read and returned the file, he was even more convinced that the man should be off the working force. During nineteen years of police work, Hamilton had gathered a total of seven justifiable homicide sheets in his record. Kinsmiller did not approve of a cop who shot first and asked questions of the corpse. True, he had killed while performing his duty, or so stated the records. But just as true was the point that three of the seven men had been unarmed. Of course, that was a fact that Hamilton could not have known, the files stated. Kinsmiller thought it might have been a point to consider before the shooting was done.

But you did not go around asking the brass to transfer cops with nineteen years of service simply because they had performed what was considered a public service. And you did not ask for transfers by saying a cop was no good after that many years just because he was starting to foul up a few simple cases. The transfer, if it came, had to come at Hamilton's request. That, or Kinsmiller had to instigate departmental charges of some sort, and prove them, and have Hamilton busted off the force.

You couldn't very well file a charge like antagonizing the squad, or inconsiderate noisemaking. Kinsmiller did not like the idea anyway. He would like to get rid of Hamilton, but he'd like to do it without making a mark on the man's record. His decision then was to wait with some tolerant understanding and hope that Hamilton did not push the pressure around the station to a point where he had to choose between filing charges

10

or losing some of his other men. And he could also wait until Hamilton blew a big case, not that he wanted him to.

But with all his tolerant understanding there was no getting around the fact that Hamilton was a prick. He was a headache that Kinsmiller didn't need along with the million or so others he already had in running the station house. He hoped fervently that Hamilton made his trip to hell alone and didn't drag any of the good cops with him when he went. There wasn't much doubt but that was where he was going, though it had taken him nineteen years to make the trip.

Kinsmiller listened to the irritating key-pecking outside his office, and walked across the room to the steel-grilled windows. He enjoyed watching the city's skyline materialize against the sunrise. Kinsmiller was a tall man with a heavy look that was accented by a stomach that was beginning to sag and trousers that had a too-tight look across the rump, a point that he had not noticed yet. Muscular in the arms and chest, with a square-jawed face and graying hair that he wore clipped short, he was beginning to show wrinkles around his dark eyes and tended to squint now from long hours of paper work. He watched the city outside with interest.

Most people say the city is black and white, with the varying shades of gray. But Kinsmiller saw the colors that were there as the sun came up. First the lightening purple as the deep shadows faded. Then the smoky blues of the city's smoke, still holding the cool night colors. Next would be the warm earth colors of brick and the soft tans on the different faces of concrete. Only in the sun's full glare was the city starkly barren, with hard lines and reflecting glass stabbing at the eyes.

But by then Kinsmiller was always too busy to notice. He watched now with enjoyment and became dimly aware of a

11

telephone ringing insistently in the squad room. When the telephone on his desk rang a few minutes later, he resented the intrusion. He crossed to the desk and lifted the receiver, saying, "Kinsmiller. What is it?"

The desk sergeant in the squad room said, "We got a squeal from the patrolman on Sunset Avenue, Lieutenant."

"Yes?"

"It's a homicide, Lieutenant. Patrolman says some woman's been murdered."

Kinsmiller sighed patiently. "Well, send someone down and tell them to call in when they can."

"I can't."

Kinsmiller stared at the instrument in his hand. "Why in hell can't you?"

"Lieutenant, there ain't nobody here to send."

"That's a little hard to believe," Kinsmiller said. "I find it damn hard to believe that at a quarter to five in the morning, when there should be two shifts of detectives out there, you can't find one to answer a homicide squeal." He paused, breathing hard. "Where in hell is everybody around here when you need them?"

"The graveyard shift is out on a squeal in Fairlawn," the sergeant offered.

"That helps."

"And the relief ain't due for fifteen minutes yet. They're out for coffee."

"And who in hell is typing out there? Machine Gun Kelly?"

"Just Hamilton's here."

"So send Hamilton. He *is* a cop, you know. He *does* work

here." The lieutenant could hear the typewriter clicking in the background.

"Well, well, how about you coming out here and sending him, Lieutenant? I just answer the phone around here."

"What the hell is this?"

"I already asked him if he wanted to take the squeal."

"And?"

"He said no, he's not on duty yet."

"Oh, Jesus Christ," Kinsmiller said.

"He told me to take a flying intercourse at a rolling donut, but that ain't the way he said it." The sergeant sounded a little miffed.

"Send that son-of-a-bitch in here," Kinsmiller said. "No, wait a minute, I'll be right out." He slammed the phone down and headed for the door.

Hamilton was still patiently typing at his desk when Kinsmiller entered the room. He was as tall as the lieutenant, a big, hard man who dressed sloppily and always seemed to have his tie loose and his hat on crooked, and, as often as not, there was a spot of coffee or a smear of cigarette ashes on the white shirt under the open jacket.

It irritated Kinsmiller, though he didn't much care if his men wore jackboots and jockey shorts as the uniform of the day, as long as they did their jobs.

Kinsmiller riveted his gaze on the man and started across the room. There was a relaxed air about Hamilton that created a false impression of slowness. He was, in reality, as quick with his hands and feet as a Mexican purse snatcher with a skinful of pep pills.

Hamilton looked up from his typing and watched the

13

lieutenant's approach with a pair of cold green eyes that were tight and narrow, matching his thin mouth. He had a complexion like an old glove. It was well used and pitted in places by scars from flying glass and sharp finger rings. There was a white ribbon of scar tissue starting on the left side of his cleft chin and following the jawline back to a point directly below the ear. It was there as a reminder of the difference between the quick and the dead. He had been quick when a drunk tried to cut his throat with a broken beer bottle while Hamilton was attempting to break up a bar fight on Sunset. The man who had tried it was now dead; that was the difference. The scar helped remind Hamilton to be even quicker in the future.

Hamilton did not have what is sometimes termed a well-rounded education. He had been in the lower third of his class at the police academy back when the physical qualifications for being a cop were the ability to hear thunder and see lightning. If you could do that, you were in, and your education was completed by being assigned to a beat on Sunset Avenue. Hamilton, you might say, graduated from a school where the only bad marks you received were from a dirty sock full of ball bearings behind the ear or a pool cue through your guts in some dark alley. He had learned his lesson well. He knew everything about crime and punks that counted.

And, to round out his education, he also knew the state's penal code and the rules and regulations of the police force. He was weighing his knowledge of the force's regulations as he watched the lieutenant stop before his desk.

"All right," Kinsmiller said. "What's going on out here?"

"Is something going on?" Hamilton asked.

"Didn't I hear that a homicide squeal just came in here?"

14

"I heard it mentioned," Hamilton said. "The sergeant asked me to take it."

"And what did you tell him?"

"I told him to take a flying f—"

"Never mind," Kinsmiller said evenly, and glanced at the clock above the door. It was seven minutes to five. "Now *I'm* asking you to answer the squeal. What are you going to tell *me?*"

Hamilton judged the weight that his years on the force carried, judged the younger man's rank, and said, "Be reasonable, Lieutenant. That goddamn squeal came in on the graveyard shift. I've got enough troubles with what happens when I'm on duty."

"You're on duty twenty-four hours a day," Kinsmiller said. "I don't have to tell you that. I'm running this goddamn station, and I'm telling you to take that squeal!"

"Twenty-four hours, huh?"

Kinsmiller watched him.

"Does that mean I have to sleep with my pistol too, Lieutenant?"

"Are you going to take that squeal?"

Hamilton rose and picked up his hat from the desk. "All right," he said. "I don't know why you're getting so hot over a lousy homicide. She can wait a few minutes. She's dead, ain't she?"

"Maybe that's why I'm hot," Kinsmiller said tersely. "I want someone to do something about it."

"I'll call in," Hamilton said. He put on his hat and patted the shoulder holster holding his .38 against his chest. He walked casually along the partition that divided the squad room from the booking room.

15

"Let me know how it is," he told the desk sergeant as he went by.

"Huh? How what is?"

Hamilton turned and made a vulgar motion with his hands. "With the donut," he said, and went out.

The city was awake in the morning sun when Hamilton reached Sunset Avenue. Death has a tranquilizing effect when it is viewed in the brightness of a new sun. It is an effect that reaches out and spreads itself by whispers, touching curious crowds on the sidewalk, stopping a day worker with a cold chill and stilling the whistle on his lips, reaching out into the buildings themselves and pulling silent, staring faces to the windows to look and feel surprise that death has been so near, unheard and unexpected. It stilled the new day's early babble and crept down the avenue to cause pursed lips and shrugged shoulders.

Death gave people something to think about.

Hamilton thought about it as an unwarranted misery that would, and already had, upset his day. He double-parked his car beside the patrol car that blocked the alley and walked casually through the litter to the group of patrolmen and lab technicians gathered at a collection of garbage cans at the rear of the Swan Bar.

"Who called in?"

One of the bulls pointed. "Stanley, over there."

Hamilton jerked his head in a come-along fashion at Stanley and walked to where the girl lay. The flies were already showing interest in the blackish pool of blood under the girl's head.

"Fill me in," he told Stanley.

The patrolman repeated the sequence of events that led

16

him to the body and finished with, "You'd think someone would have heard her screaming back here." He glanced at the waiting men.

No one answered.

Stanley avoided looking at the body. "It looks like a rape, don't it?" He directed the question at Hamilton.

"Look again," Hamilton urged, and stared at him. "How long you been down here?"

"On this beat?"

"Yeah, on this beat."

"Six months, I guess."

"You must be taking stupid pills then," Hamilton observed. "You could ax your grandmother to death in the middle of the street at noon down here, and nobody would see or hear you." He pointed at the body. "And as for rape, I don't see how it looks like rape yet."

"Well, she's undressed," Stanley said. "And I don't see any underclothes around."

"Tell me something," Hamilton said. "What's a good reason for a woman to be in an alley down here, and not have any pants on? A live one, that is."

"You riding me?"

"I asked you a question."

Stanley eyed Hamilton warily. "I can't see any reason. Why?"

"I just thought that a cop with your vast experience on this beat would know that most of the hookers down here leave their pants in the dresser when they go to work. It ain't quality down here, it's quantity, and these hookers will run a guy back here for a two-dollar quickie. They don't have time to fool with underclothes for a two-buck curb service off the top of a gar-

17

bage can." Hamilton paused, then continued sweetly: "Now that you've had your sex education for the day, you have maybe learned something. Besides that, it's hot out. Who says a girl's got to wear a bra and pants anyway?"

"It just looks . . . looks like rape, don't it? It *could* be rape, couldn't it?" He stared at Hamilton belligerently. "What do you think?"

"I don't think," Hamilton said. "I've just worked around here for a while. I know what I see right now—I see a body. That's all. Maybe rape. Maybe not. Why borrow trouble and jump to conclusions?"

"Yeah, but what do you call it right now?"

"I call it like a hooker's had some trouble servicing one of her customers. That's how I call it."

He looked at the two ambulance men and rubbed his hands together. "How about you two ghouls giving me a hand before the flies get her," he said. "I don't have a partner on this squeal."

Nobody in the group wondered why.

In his apartment on East Floral, Chuck Rawls was wondering why Friday always seemed to be the day when everything went wrong. During the rest of the week he could at least depend on having coffee with his usual eggs and toast for breakfast.

This was Friday. And just for spite the coffeepot had boiled over, putting out the gas burner, so that the kitchenette now reeked of gas. It had happened while he showered and shaved. The pop-up toaster had also decided not to pop up his toast and had instead charred it to look like an Aztec sun offering.

18

All things considered, it was probably a good thing he had forgotten to buy eggs last night. He always burned them on Friday too.

A full stomach makes a patient man, he thought. His mother had told him that. If that was the case, he should work out of a restaurant, because if any job needed patience, his did. He sat at the small table and sipped the almost coffee he'd made. He would have an early lunch, he decided, glancing at the clock above the stove. His first appointment was at nine o'clock. It would give him some time to review the man's case history once more.

He rose from the chair and carried the wreckage of breakfast to the sink. Rawls was a small man, with delicate hands and the whipcord-hard body of a bullfighter. His hair was red, clipped short but still appearing as if it had been styled in a wind tunnel. He had a fair complexion and bright blue eyes. In all, his appearance tended to make him look younger than his twenty-five years. His boyish looks were an asset when he talked to one of his younger parolees. He was of the new school, his looks implied. Therefore, he might understand. But that was a two-ended stick. His older cases, the men with long records and a few trips to prison behind them, tended to view him as a wet-eared punk. The unspoken attitude then was: What can this kid tell me? He had a lot of cases, well over a hundred. Some of the parolees, young and old, thought of him as "that redheaded kid who's going to try to save the world by tomorrow." Quite a few of them called him other things.

With the dishes stacked, he picked up his hat and brief-case from the couch in the living room and went down to his car. He knew that the morning traffic would be heavy downtown. It would be a madhouse past Adams Drive during the morning rush. And though there was little to be thankful for in working at the Slade County Courthouse, he was grateful that parole agents were assigned parking places.

He drove west on Floral toward the downtown section of the city, moving parallel to Sunset Avenue, six blocks to the north. Living on Floral was as though he'd subconsciously picked an apartment on the front line of what was considered the city proper, and that part of the city unofficially known as Little Budapest, because of the street fighting that seemed to erupt there weekly. He liked to be close to his work. And in an area of two hundred and seventy blocks he had plenty of work.

For once, his parking place behind the courthouse had not been borrowed by a visiting bondsman, or an attorney. He crossed the parking lot with the sun beating strongly against his back, reminding him that his office would be sun-baked until noon, and by then the whole building would be hot.

It was still cool in the long corridors on the first floor of the courthouse. The halls were spotlessly clean, and smelled of disinfectant. He admired the smooth marble under his feet. Here, at least, they see things clean and orderly, he thought. A sample of directed effort.

Sure, he added. And they call it Big Brother's workshop. I wonder if any parolees would ever come down here voluntarily for advice. There was a cheerlessness in the thought that depressed him. He considered good advice as destructive as bad advice when it had to be forced down a man's throat. It was the reason that he visited his parolees at their homes or places of work whenever he could. He wanted to help them; that's why he'd taken the job.

You could call him naïve, or square if you wanted to, but

20

the fact was he liked helping people. There was no such word as incorrigible in his personal dictionary. People are worth helping. It was as simple as that.

His office was at the end of the first right-hand corridor at the back of the building. He glanced at his watch as he reached the door and entered. He had a half hour yet before his first appointment.

The office was a duplicate of the ten other parole agents' offices along the corridor, a rectangle with three wide windows on the sunny side of the room. His desk sat in front of the center window, a file cabinet on the right, a coat rack on the left. To the left of the door, as you entered, there were four wooden chairs and a sand-filled ashtray. There was a twelve-inch fan on top of the file cabinet.

He crossed the room and switched on the fan. Then opened the three windows as he moved toward the coat rack. And reaching that, he hung his coat and hat before turning to his desk. It was a routine he had followed for seven months.

The file on William Knudson was in his center desk drawer, where he'd left it the night before. He placed it on the desk before him and looked up at the plaque hanging directly across from him on the door. He had placed it where he would always see it in looking up. He did not want to forget his job. There were parole agents who did.

Without seeing the words, he read:

The descent to Avernus is easy; the gate of Pluto open night and day; but to retrace one's steps and return to the upper air, that is the toil, that the difficulty.

VIRGIL

Then he said aloud, "And I think that I'm making the trip with them." He glanced down at the file before him and

21

sighed deeply. Sometimes he felt like a computer. This is re-habilitation machine Chuck Rawls, folks. Just feed in the case's vital information and a case solution will result immediately.

Sure it will. There are several parole programs right there in that file cabinet. One of them could be tailored to fit each need or case history. And after that, it was a matter of seeing that the man kept to the program.

Or he violated his parole. And there was always one coming out to try the tailored programs, and going back, and coming out again, and going back. . . .

He knew what was wrong with him. It was Friday, and he had lost another man that week. There was nothing un-usual about that, he guessed. He had seen a lot of violation forms go out of his office. And that was just what was wrong.

He wondered why.

Why should it happen? I'm doing everything I can. The truth is that I probably give a parolee more breaks than the other agents do. I'm known as a soft touch. I like my work. I like the idea of what I'm doing to get a man back to a normal life. So why do the violations keep going out of here? He did not like sending one of his men back.

It showed a failure on his part, he felt. It was like saying, "Here he is. I couldn't reach him. So lock him up again." Failure and waste. He'd already seen too much of that.

He didn't like either one. He had a hundred and twenty-seven chances of failure in his files. Too many. And that many chances of success, he reminded himself.

He flipped open the new file and began to read. How do I reach you, mister? How do I keep you out here so I don't feel like I'm sending a part of myself to prison if you go back? How do I understand you? How do I keep you out?

22

They were all good questions. But there were some people in the city who were thinking along opposite lines.

By the time that William Knudson was scheduled to show up at Rawls' office, a police call was being sent out from the East Bagley station to the working bulls. It was a simple pick-up-and-hold-for-questioning call directed at men with a record of sex offenses.

It was routine.

There had been a murder in the city last night.

There had also been a rape committed during that murder last night.

Today there would be a pervert parade. . . . It was as simple as that.

3

There always seemed to be a million things to do on a murder case. It is a compounded mess when rape is added as a possible motive for murder. It helped like hell if you knew who had been murdered and raped. Hamilton had asked for a pre-autopsy opinion from the medical examiner who answered the squeal in the alley behind the Swan Bar. He had got one. Now he would have liked to know who the corpse was.

Sometimes you had to wait for fingerprints to learn a corpse's identity, and at other times the missing persons office had to be checked and someone called in to identify the body. And too, there were times when nothing worked, and you were left with the job of finding a killer of an unknown corpse, which can get pretty difficult.

Hamilton was not worried about not knowing yet who she was. Dead or not, to Hamilton a woman was begging for it if she started working Sunset Avenue. She was practically asking for a buzzing if she pulled that quickie-in-the-alley service. There had been a lot of hooker-buzzing done on the avenue that summer. It appeared that the punks had gone a little too far this time in the fine art of rolling a whore. It annoyed Hamilton that he would have to spend some time questioning a bunch of punks because they made their summer recreation money by purse-snatching and whore-buzzing. Only on the second activity did they usually steal more than money.

He also was annoyed that the medical examiner had seen it as a possible rape. Because of that, he would now have to talk to a bunch of perverts. He had called the station house and given them the good news. The sex offenders would be picked up and held for questioning. Hamilton would rather question them somewhere on the avenue where he could be alone with them and thereby ensure some degree of truth in their answers. While he did not like punks in general, he disliked sex offenders in particular. He was greatly annoyed with the squeal from any angle he looked at it. There were just too many possibilities and he didn't even know her name yet.

He sat on the back steps of the Swan Bar and watched the lab boys taking the alley apart like a foursome of demented garbage collectors. There were eight garbage cans next to the chalked outline where the girl's body had been. The lab boys were now emptying the cans, piece by piece. They were looking for a possible murder weapon.

Hamilton hoped that they found it, preferably with nice clear fingerprints. Instead, they found the girl's purse. There was a very nice identification card in the purse. There was also a photo of the murdered girl. Both were powdered for fingerprints and the powder transferred to foil before the lab boys handed them over to Hamilton, first having extracted a receipt for them.

The identification card served only to annoy Hamilton further. It was certainly not going to be his day. He had got a case that wasn't his, and it had turned out to be one that had as many suspects as the avenue had creeps. And now it had become confusing. Hamilton had been wrong.

Mary Blair was not a hooker. Her apartment address was

25

over on Adams Drive, which was nowhere near where she had been found. It was confusing to Hamilton just what a welfare worker would be doing down on the avenue, in the early morning hours, dressed, or undressed, like a whore.

He considered the identification card. The pervert parade would be a good place to start on this one, he decided. He was glad that Stanley was not around to remind him that his first guess had been wrong. Well, a man could be wrong sometimes, he decided. So she wasn't a whore.

He had called it like he'd seen it. Any of them whiz kid detectives on the squad would have called it the same way—a hooker who had thrown herself into trouble.

She wasn't though.

So what in hell was she doing down here then? he wondered. He put the card and photo into his pocket, waved a mocking salute at the still busy lab technicians, and walked down the alley toward the street.

Why was she down here in this hole?

Hamilton reached the sidewalk and stood looking along the avenue. It was his part of the city. He'd pounded its sidewalks and alleys when he'd worn a bull's uniform. And he'd cruised it after he'd put on a suit. He could take care of himself down here. He understood punks. He struck first, and often.

The punks on the avenue knew him, the citizens he was there to protect knew him. He had that cop look. Both the punks and the citizens stayed out of his way. He had built a reputation on the avenue, and nobody wanted Hamilton on their backs.

He leaned against a light pole and watched the citizens with hooded eyes. The punks are here because they live in this hole, he thought. And they blame cops for it being a hole, and

26

for every lump they get. But they stay, and keep on getting lumps. I'm here because someone has to give out the lumps. Now why in hell was Mary Blair here?

Welfare workers don't run around trying to save humanity during the early morning hours. There was damn little to save down here anyway. But she could have been one of those dewy-eyed college kids who run around spouting love and understanding. He had read that theory more than once. A firm hand and an understanding attitude was their solution to this hole. A blackjack party and tougher judges were more like it.

Hamilton lit a cigarette. Well, now she knew just what that love-and-understanding theory would get you down here. It had got her dead. That fine, forgiving attitude got you nothing but crap rubbed in your face. Nobody could understand that. But then, nobody understood punks like Hamilton did.

They should see half the crap that I do, he thought. Then they wouldn't be so goddamn understanding that it killed them. I would certainly like to know who she was down here trying to save, if she was. That's the trouble with love-and-understanding people. They're the type that keep half these punks out of a cell where they belong. Or in a padded cell where they belong. People like that would let the animals out of a zoo if they could.

Well, now one of those animals had murdered and raped again. Now he had to catch him. And when he did, they'd probably turn him loose.

I hope this rape-o is a wise punk, he thought. I hope he gives me some crap when I get him, and I will get him. I hope he gives me some excuse to blow him away. He grinned at the thought. That's one cure for crime that they can't get a re-

27

prieve from. So, rape-o, I know all about the terrible mental state that makes you do something like what they found in that alley. I'll cure that for you too, if you give me an excuse.

He flipped his cigarette into the street and walked up the sidewalk to his car. The ID card had given him more than her name. It had also listed the address of the office where she worked.

He wiped the sweat from his face as he got into the car. A welfare office was as good a place as any to start a murder investigation, he guessed. The pervert parade could wait.

Frankie Trumper was a pervert.

He had once looked the word up in a dictionary in the prison library. He had found:

pervert (per vert′), *v.* 1. To lead or turn from the right way. 2. To give a wrong meaning to. 3. To use for the wrong purposes. 4. To change from what is natural or normal. **Syn.** Corrupt, debase, deprave.

Frankie had thought about it. He could not see where there was anything unnatural about wanting a little piece of tail. That was normal as hell. And he hadn't corrupted anyone. He had reluctantly admitted that he might be a rape-o all right, but he wasn't a pervert.

That wasn't so bad.

It had been bad enough to make him serve four years of a twenty-year sentence at the state prison for all his insisting that it hadn't really been a crime of violence. He hadn't hurt the girl, had he? The parole board must have wondered how much fight a fifteen-year-old can put up. He served four of the twenty, he would serve the other sixteen on parole if he kept his nose clean.

28

Frankie had been out for six months, and he was keeping his nose as clean as he could. He lay on the cot in his room and watched a cockroach marching its way across the ceiling.

There was the cot, a small dresser, and a wooden chair in the room, a cheap radio set on the chair beside the cot. There was a window in the wall facing the door of the room. The view from the third floor was the blank wall of the next building and the alley between the two. The room was a so-called sleeping room, according to the landlady. It was perhaps nine feet wide and twelve feet long. It cost Frankie five dollars a week.

That was a lot of money when you made thirty-six fifty a week, after deductions. It had been a mistake taking that dishwashing job. From three to nine, yet. He wouldn't stay there a second if he wasn't on parole. A goddamn paper prison, that's what parole was.

The difference was that you're the screw out here, he thought. You're the keeper. You tell yourself, Frankie get up, Frankie go to work. Don't stop for a beer. Be a good boy, Frankie. That's what that boy wonder Rawls said. You're doing good, Frankie. No trouble. No problems. You're doing fine.

The boy wonder wouldn't know a problem if it bit him in the ass, he thought. Stupid. Stupid. That's what he was. A lousy hypocrite with his "I want to help you" line. That wet-nosed bastard just didn't want any problems; he'd crucify you if you farted wrong.

Frankie sat up on the cot and threw a magazine at the cockroach. He reached over and turned the radio off, thinking about Rawls. You pious bastard, you should live in this hole. You really helped me with that job too. Some job. I got to kick back five bucks a week to that greasy slob who runs the place. There's a lot of guys looking for work, he says. So you kick back a fin a week and we'll get along. You don't kick back and I'll tell that nice parole agent I caught you with your hand in the till. Why'd Rawls think that greasy slob was so willing to hire an ex-con anyway? Everybody has got to live, he says. Sure, so I got to get stuck on a job where I can't help but meet that bitch.

You're doing fine, Frankie.

That's how much Rawls knew. He could hear the distant wail of a police siren, and he tensed on his cot until it faded. His sweat stank of fear, and his hands shook as he lit a cigarette.

Frankie knew he was in trouble over the girl.

During the six months he'd been out, he had learned that having a sex beef on your record was like having a brother on the force; he was down to the station house that often. It was as sure as fate: let one woman, even the biggest hooker around, holler rape, and you might just as well put on your best suit, because there was going to be a trip down to the station to stand in a lineup.

But this time it wasn't just a sex rap. This was a big one. A chance to go to the death house if some honest citizen fingered you in a lineup.

Were there any witnesses? he wondered. Nothing had been said about a witness during the early newscast. But the cops might keep it quiet if there was. He had better not take any chances by wearing the same clothes he'd had on last night.

He rose from the cot and walked to the dresser. He was a solid man with a weight lifter's build and a dark Latin face that made people wonder why he had to be a rape-o. He had

30

black wavy hair and dark eyes that had a slight Oriental slant. He could have been mistaken for a Puerto Rican or a Cuban, and sometimes was. Everybody knew that when a woman fingered a man in a lineup for rape, she usually fingered a Puerto Rican or a Cuban, or a Negro; or she fingered Frankie.

As he dressed, the fear came back. He wouldn't be surprised if the police were on their way over right now. His fear built a dryness in his mouth. He hadn't been very careful last night. Not like before. He couldn't concentrate on being careful when he felt like that.

He felt cold and scared when he finished dressing.

How much should I tell them? he wondered.

The bulls weren't stupid. They'd find out where she worked. And they already knew where he worked. They wouldn't have to be very smart to find out that she came in there sometimes. Smart uppity bitch, coming into a slop house like that, like she was one of the crowd, and smiling at everybody while she twitched around in those maidenly skirts she wore. She'd even smiled at him the first time they'd met, like he was a friend instead of a lousy dishwasher and delivery boy. That bitch really had an act.

So the cops would find out she came in there, he decided. I'll play it dumb, like I don't know Miss Fancy Pants from Adam. I seen her in there a few times. That's all he'd tell them.

He could give them cops an earful about Mary Blair. He could fool the bastards and go right down to the station now, saying how he'd heard about it over the radio and had some information on her. She was no better than any other bitch, for all her sweet, innocent act.

And the cops would say . . .

They would say, How come you know so much about her,

31

Frankie? Were you following her around? How about that? Did you like her legs or her walk best? Did you just want to touch her, Frankie? That's what the cops would say. They'd never believe it like it was.

They would bring up that other time. Remember how you just wanted to touch that other girl, Frankie? Tell us all about this information you're so anxious to give us.

Frankie was sweating; the sweat darkened the new shirt and made his hands slick. Yeah, that's what they'd say, all right. And when they were done, he'd be back in the pen.

Besides, that stupid Rawls would probably violate his parole if he found out about the other things. That lousy kid ran a tough paper prison for all his spouting how much he wanted to help a guy.

He shook his head. He had to take it easy. He couldn't act nervous when they picked him up. He had to act surprised and play the game right. He had to act like he didn't know a thing about what the cops asked, and he'd better go ahead and do just what he'd do on any other day. He would go eat.

There was a drugstore on the corner of Sixteenth and Lexington, a half block away from his rooming house. At the back of the store there was a lunch counter. There was a newsstand on the sidewalk in front of the store where you could place a bet on a pony or play the numbers, and if the owner of the stand knew your face he could probably find a few dirty pictures or a pack of marijuana cigarettes for you. He also sold things like information to the cops. Frankie had not even had time to finish his coffee and read the comic section of the newspaper when the bulls picked him up. He knew it was going to be a long day.

There was a sign on the second building off the corner of Twelfth and Sunset. It was the only thing that set the building apart from the rest of the block. The sign was a businesslike white-on-black directory.

It read:

SLADE COUNTY WELFARE BRANCH   3
SOCIAL CENTER   1
CLINIC   2
CHILD WELFARE   3
YOUTH REHABILITATION   4

Hamilton trekked up the chipped concrete steps, read the sign, and climbed the inside steps to the door on the third floor where a sign told him that Mr. Martin Grewe was supervisor of welfare. He pushed through the door.

The third floor of the building was a single large room that had been partitioned off into many small penlike areas. They reminded Hamilton of stock pens, except that in each pen there were a desk, three chairs, and a small file cabinet, instead of an assortment of stock. And each pen had a cardboard sign to identify its female occupant. It was a very businesslike setup.

On the pen nearest to the door there was a sign that clearly ordered "STOP HERE FIRST," and another identifying Miss Kenton as the occupant of the pen.

It was a great place for signs, Hamilton decided. He followed directions, walked over to Miss Kenton's pen, and stood waiting patiently until the woman looked up and smiled.

"Yes?" she asked. She had a rather plain face until she smiled. She was a slender woman of about thirty, with hazel eyes, sand-brown hair, and freckles, which is a pretty average combination. But she was one of those people who smile as if they mean it. There was none of this just-the-lips smiling for Miss Kenton. Her entire face smiled; even her eyes smiled as if they'd just discovered sunlight or something and thought it was simply wonderful. It made you think of a girl-next-door poster.

It made Hamilton's day for him. You just don't get that kind of a smile very often when you're a cop. It was a smile that was full of softness and warmth. And these are pretty rare qualities to turn up in his day. And because he didn't really believe there were any women of the girl-next-door type left in the city, he was almost sure she would vanish when he spoke.

"Miss Kenton," he said. There was a note of amazement in his voice, and she smiled again, and repeated, "Yes?"

"I'm from the police," he said. "I'm Detective Hamilton. I'd like to see Mr. Grewe."

The smile clouded a little. "We received a call about Mary only an hour ago," she said. "Is this about her?"

"Mary Blair?"

She nodded.

"It's about her," he said.

She reached for the phone on her desk, stopped, folded her hands, and asked softly, "May I see your identification, please?"

Hamilton sighed and took out his wallet, opening it to where his badge was pinned.

"There were two newspapermen here already this morning," she explained. "Mr. Grewe asked me to keep them out." She picked up the phone and pushed a button below the dial.

"Mr. Grewe," she said, watching Hamilton and smiling again. "The police are here now, a Detective Hamilton."

She listened for a moment.

"Yes, sir," she said, and put the phone back in its cradle. "Go right in. All the way back, turn right past Mrs. Maxwell's desk; there's a door there."

Hamilton made the turn past Mrs. Maxwell's desk and opened the door there. The room was a larger replica of the pens. There were a desk, three chairs, and a large file cabinet. There was also a single leather couch against one wall. The couch proved that position had its privileges, Hamilton imagined.

Grewe was a harassed-appearing man in his late fifties with a completely bald head and patient eyes. He wore a pair of thick glasses set down low on his nose, and peered at Hamilton over them as he came from behind the desk and extended his hand.

"This is a terrible thing, Detective Hamilton," he said as they shook hands.

Hamilton wondered if Grewe expected him to say, Indeed it is, Supervisor Grewe. Instead, he said, "It happens."

"Is it true that she was attacked?"

"She was murdered," Hamilton said dryly. "That's enough."

"Yes. Of course. But to be molested too. A young girl like that. Do the police have any idea . . ."

"I just got here, Mr. Grewe," Hamilton said. "With some help from you, we might have some ideas."

"Yes. Certainly," Grewe said. "Sit down. Take the couch there; it's quite comfortable." He waited until Hamilton was seated before he went back to his chair behind the desk. He smiled at Hamilton. "Now then," he said. "What can I do to help you?"

Hamilton took out his notebook. "Tell me about Mary Blair for a start."

"What about her?" Grewe asked. "I mean what in particular? I'm afraid I don't know much about her personal life."

"Her job. What exactly was her job here?"

"She was one of our case workers in the DCA field. She enjoyed working with children."

"DCA?"

"Dependent Children Aid," Grewe said. "Her cases were those where a girl has one or more children and no means of support."

"No husband, you mean?"

"Well, in some cases there has been a separation in the family. In other cases, the children are illegitimate. In all cases, the girl must identify the children's father before being eligible for DCA."

Sounds like a gravy train for hookers who slipped, Hamilton thought. He said, "She must have come in contact with a lot of people then. How many cases like that did she have?"

"All of our girls have more cases than they should," Grewe said. "Mary had at least thirty-five. I'd have to check. And she always took an extra interest in the Path."

"The social center downstairs?"

"Yes, we were just getting that started when she came to work for us. It's been about three years now. She was one of its strongest supporters, always willing to do extra work there." He paused. "We don't pay our girls for the youth center work; it's a volunteer project."

36

"And she volunteered for that too, huh?" Hamilton asked. "Beside handling more than thirty DCA cases."

"The youth center is a very important project with us here," Grewe said. "It's just what the young people from this district need, we feel."

Hamilton knew what the punks needed.

"When did you last see Miss Blair alive, Mr. Grewe?"

"About five last night. I still find it difficult to believe—"

"Tell me about it."

"Well, the others were leaving for the day, and Mary stopped in here to tell me that she had picked up the extra key to the center. She came in and we chatted about the dance."

"Why did she want the key?"

"To open the center for the dance, of course," Grewe said. "It was our fall dance. It gives the kids a place to—"

"Hold it," Hamilton said. "She chaperoned a dance here last night. Is that it?"

"Yes, our fall dance," Grewe said. "It was to start at eight."

"And last until when?"

"The center closes at eleven, because of the curfew, you know. She would have made sure the children had time to get home before then."

"Then she left at five and returned to chaperon the dance at eight. Did she?"

"Did she what?"

"Chaperon the dance?"

"Of course. I called the center at nine and she assured me that everything was fine. She was chaperoning alone, you know, and sometimes the kids get a little rowdy. So I called her at nine."

37

"You said five o'clock was the last time you'd seen her alive."

"It was. I called her at nine."

"Don't get technical," Hamilton said. "Nine o'clock, then, was the last time you *knew* she was alive."

"Yes."

"Did she close the center at eleven then?"

"I'm sure I don't know. I would imagine she did. She was always very good at things like that. The kids would know."

"Where is the key she had?"

Grewe stared at him, paused, then picked up the phone and asked Miss Kenton to check the key board. While they waited, he said, "The doors can be opened from the inside without the key. The girls usually put the key back on the board once they open the center, then they simply close the doors when they leave." He smiled weakly. "Less chance of losing a key then." He listened to Miss Kenton's voice a moment before he put down the phone and said, "The key isn't there."

"Don't you usually check on that key when you come in on the mornings after a dance?"

"I just assumed that it would be there. Mary was dependable."

Hamilton thought for a moment. "Can I get a list of her cases—the names, addresses, the works?"

"Miss Kenton will have them."

"And I'd like to talk to the rest of the girls out there. They should know who the kids were who came to the center, right?"

"Why, I suppose so. They've all been chaperons at one time or another. You don't think . . ."

38

"I don't think anything, Mr. Grewe. I'm just doing my job."

"I suppose you are," Grewe said. "You can use my office to talk to the girls."

"Fine," Hamilton said. "And I'd like to take a look at the center too, before it's cleaned up. It hasn't been, has it?"

"I don't think so," Grewe said. "The girls usually did that on their own time. It doubled as a sort of lounge for them. A volunteer thing, as I said." He paused. "I can check."

"Do that."

Grewe looked at his watch, then up at the door. "If you're finished with me, I could have one of the girls come in."

"There's a few more things," Hamilton said.

"Yes?"

"Where were *you* last night, Mr. Grewe?"

Grewe looked at him as though he was kidding.

Hamilton wasn't kidding a bit.

4

Ten forty-five A.M. was the time that Rawls usually took his morning coffee break. By then the sun had reached its high, brassy glare and the streets outside had taken on a mirage appearance, distorted, like an ever-changing painting done on hot glass.

Rawls looked at the streets from his office window. It really isn't that hot, he told himself. It's the glare that suggests the heat. The power of suggestion. Think cool, boy. Think of waterfalls, with a clear deep pool and green trees just oozing shade and coolness. Think of snow, cool—cool snow against your face.

God damn! It is hot in this office!

That's because it's Friday. The day just hadn't started out right. It was bad enough when he had to violate a man's parole after he'd worked with him, but to violate a parole without ever meeting the parolee was too much. It could only happen on a Friday.

He had waited until nine-thirty for William Knudson to show up for his first interview. Then he had called Knudson's home. He was not there, and he had not been there.

"But he was released from prison yesterday afternoon," Rawls had said. "It's only thirty miles from here."

"I know how far it is," Knudson's father had informed

him. "He still ain't here. So how about calling somewhere else and looking for him? I work nights. I never should have told him to come back here anyway."

Rawls had called the prison next. They knew exactly where Knudson was. He was in cell 326 of G cell block. He was something of a celebrity around there. He had served the shortest parole that they knew of. Knudson had served five years for check-writing—or drunken driving with a fountain pen, as the man at the prison said. They had given him a new suit, his parole papers, and twenty dollars promptly at noon yesterday.

He celebrated his freedom by stopping at the roadhouse a half mile from the prison gates. He had celebrated twenty dollars' worth. And being out of funds to continue his celebration, he had flexed his fingers, and asked the owner for a pen and a blank check. A member of the parole board had walked into the roadhouse at the time he was getting his check cashed.

William Knudson had been a free man for approximately two hours.

He even got his old cell back.

Rawls didn't believe it.

A call to the parole board assured him it was true. He was probably the first agent to write out a "violated" form without having the opportunity to meet the man. It was a distinction he could do without.

He had wondered why, and asked himself what could possibly happen next. Then he had turned his attention to the reports from the men he'd seen on Thursday. He tried to match each man's monthly report with the memory of his last visit with the man. A thing that might appear to be a very simple process unless you remembered that he was visited in his office by more than a hundred men each month, each an individual case, and unless you knew that he tried to visit each of his cases away from the office each month. He usually managed to visit only half of them, which meant that he saw each of his cases away from the office every other month. And when it came right down to the problem, it could get confusing as hell just who was who in your files.

He worked at that until Eberhart, from the office next to his, opened the door and asked if he was a state man or if he was going out for coffee. He was.

He finished putting on his jacket, glanced apprehensively at the phone, and was starting around the desk as it rang. He returned to the desk and picked it up. "Rawls," he said.

"Glad I caught you, Chuck," Herb Cochan's voice said. "I thought you might be headed for the Derby."

"I was on my way," Rawls said. "You just caught me. What does the head man of Little Budapest's gestapo want this morning?"

"You're starting to talk like your parolees," Cochan said. "Besides, you have it wrong. Cops are the Gestapo down there; parole agents are called Big Brother."

Rawls smiled to himself. "Well, what do they call the head man of Big Brother then?"

"How's Chief District Parole Agent sound?"

"I can see you're not in a very humorous mood this morning," Rawls said. "What's up anyway?"

"Can you come over to my office a minute?"

"Sure."

"Fine," Cochan said. "I'll tell you then." He hung up and Rawls stared at the phone, then at his watch. He was going to miss coffee for sure. And that was par for the course on Friday.

42

Cochan's office was next to the records room near the center of the building. Cochan himself was a man whose appearance reminded everybody of files and dusty ledgers. One expected to find him standing behind a high English pulpit with a parchment volume before him, and a crow quill in his hand. He was a thin man with a long bony face and big hands. His entire body seemed to be thinness and knobby joints. There were two paper containers of coffee on his desk as Rawls entered his office. "I had some coffee sent in," he said. "This might take a while."

"Is something wrong with one of my reports?" Rawls asked, taking a chair.

"No. Nothing like that," Cochan assured him. He pushed a container toward Rawls. "Hope you like it black." He paused. "How are things going, Chuck? Getting into the routine all right?"

"I'm buried in it, right up to my ears," Rawls said. "But I'm learning. Seven months is just about enough time to take the shine off my briefcase and put it on the seat of my pants."

"Well, that's why I called you over after I checked this file." He glanced at the memo pad on his desk. "There was a pretty brutal murder committed last night. A murder-rape to be exact. One of the city's welfare workers was attacked and murdered after a dance."

Cochan paused, pried the top from his coffee container and sipped cautiously. "There's going to be one hell of a stink over it. The people are going to be screaming for an arrest, and every city employee in civil serivce or welfare work of any type is going to be yelling for someone's blood."

"The city has a competent police force," Rawls said, puzzled.

43

"Quite competent," Cochan agreed. "I'm sure they will arrest whoever is responsible. But on a thing like this we get a lot of bad publicity if the guilty party is a parolee." He sighed. "They are investigating all of the prior sex offenders, of course. One of them is Frankie Trumper; he's in your case assignment."

"I think I remember him," Rawls said. "He was paroled about the same time I took over the office alone."

"Yes, about six months ago. How much do you know about the man?"

"Well, I can't give you a case history, Herb. But from what I remember, he seems to have adjusted well. A little resentful and locked inside himself. I think I made a note of that. He's the athletic type."

"No trouble at all, huh?"

"Oh, come on, Herb. I've got a lot of guys to take care of. I've seen him five or six times, and read about that many of his monthly reports. That's what I've got to go on, and because that is all, I've got to give him a clean sheet. As far as I'm concerned, he's keeping up his end of the parole. I wouldn't violate him for getting picked up in a police dragnet, if that's what you mean."

"When would you violate him?"

"What kind of a question is that anyway?" Rawls asked. "If he broke parole I'd violate him. If he was convicted of another crime I'd violate him. If I personally saw him, or was absolutely sure he'd violated his parole, I'd send him back."

"How about a situation where the police thought he was involved in a crime, but couldn't prove it in court?"

"No."

"No, you wouldn't?"

"Herb, I happen to think that innocent until proved guilty applies to my parolees just as much as to you and me. I won't violate a man's parole on crap like being seen on the same block where a crime was committed. That's circumstantial evidence. Our courts don't convict men on it. Why should I do the same thing as convict him by sending him back?"

"Come on now, Chuck. You know as well as I that men are convicted on circumstantial evidence. Yes, some of them get court reversals later, but men do go to prison on such convictions."

"There's a difference there," Rawls said. "A jury might possibly be swayed by a good prosecutor, coupled with a poor defense. I know it happens. What I'm saying is that *I* don't violate my men without proof that they did something. *I* have to be sure they warrant a violation."

Cochan folded his hands on the desk, hiding the coffee container completely. "Just a minute ago you said you'd had just a few meetings with your men. That leaves a lot of unaccounted time, doesn't it? A lot of room for probable criminal activities that you wouldn't know about unless the police caught them. Do you consider that?"

"Let's say that I considered the possibility. True, I can't see all or know all. But if they can't be trusted they wouldn't be out. I work with what I know, and I won't send a man back on the chance that he *might* have committed a crime. That isn't showing faith in these men, that's witch-burning."

"Suppose he's smart and almost impossible to catch?" Cochan said. "We have a duty to protect society from that if we can."

"How many men like that are there?" Rawls grinned. "We punish the guilty, not the maybe guilty."

45

Cochan sighed. "I wish I were twenty-five again," he said. "Things are so damn clear then." He smiled. "Just between us, justice is a fickle bitch at best. And it's never at its best anyplace. But I called you in here because I wanted to tell you what to expect on this murder if one of your parolees is involved."

"What do I expect?"

"More than the usual pressure for us to tighten up our control of the men. A hell of a lot more, because this girl was a social worker. A lot of the pressure will come from the inside—the kind you could expect if this were a cop-killing. People will want a head to roll."

"As long as it's the right head."

"Wait a minute," Cochan broke in. "Whether you know it or not, the police files are filled with unsolved cases that were solved and reversed by the courts. I'm telling you theoretically what will happen if a parolee is picked up, questioned, and the police place a charge against him. They will ask the grand jury for an indictment. If they get one, fine. It's up to the courts then. If they don't get one"—he paused and shook his head—"well, by then half the people in this city will have him convicted because he is a parolee and there was evidence enough for the police to try for an indictment. We'll get the pressure to violate him on those grounds alone, or to find a minor reason."

Rawls tasted his coffee and set the container down carefully on the desk. "I suppose we will. Maybe the city will take a look down here and give us the men we need then. I'd love to have only about twenty cases. Then I could give a detailed report on a man's progress without guessing."

"You're not getting the point, Chuck."

46

"What's the point?"

"A lot of pressure is going to come from close to home. The department is going to get a *lot* of it."

"We've had a lot on other cases."

"This is not other cases. That's why I'm telling you this. A welfare worker is involved—one of the family, so to speak. You might have a parolee of yours involved. I only said might."

Rawls sat silently for a moment. "Then if this theoretical situation develops, what are you telling me to do?"

"Have I ever told you how to run your cases, Chuck?"

"Not yet," Rawls said, and waited.

"I'm just suggesting that you consider this situation. And come up with a reasonable solution to it. A lot of bad publicity and pressure could hurt the department."

"A wrong decision from me could be pretty bad for a man too," Rawls said.

"Not really. Sometimes a man gets violated in a case like this for his own good. He goes back to prison for a few months, until the pressure's off, and then he appears before the parole board again."

"I'm glad you're not *telling* me how to handle this situation if it came up, Herb. Because if you were, I'd have to tell you exactly what I'd do, and you can bet that public opinion and pressure wouldn't stop me from doing it."

"Yes," Cochan said. "I'm glad I don't have to tell you what to do in theoretical situations. I might have to do that someday in a real situation." He looked away from Rawls. "I wouldn't like to do that, Chuck."

"I wouldn't like for you to."

Cochan grinned. "You haven't told me yet what you'd do though."

47

"I'd do my job," Rawls said. "Pressure and opinions be damned. I happen to think I'm right when I say I won't violate a man without him being proved guilty of something."

Cochan sat silently for several minutes, then looked at his watch. "Sorry I took up your coffee break for this talk, Chuck. Just wanted to tell you about this Trumper business because you're new." He paused. "Maybe you could find out what Trumper's been doing. Spend some extra time on it." He paused again. "Just in case."

By eleven o'clock Hamilton had spent six hours on the case. It was uncomfortably warm in Grewe's office, and the combined clatter from sixteen busy typewriters in the outer office served as a further irritation. At his best, Hamilton was as tactful as a slap in the mouth with his questioning. He was not at his best when he'd finished talking to fifteen female office machines, as he saw them, and faced the sixteenth in the form of Miss Kenton.

He was, by then, full of information about Mary Blair, case worker, and Mary Blair, chaperon, and Mary Blair, angel of mercy, friend in need, and general all-round number-one girl. But he didn't know a damn thing about Mary Blair, raped and cold on a slab, or the circumstances that could possibly have put her there.

He knew she was, or had been, the perfect example of what clean living can do for you in the eyes of your co-workers. She had been sweet, understanding, quietly devoted, and a sensible girl. She had been full of love and understanding for the world.

Hamilton didn't believe it. Virtues such as those did not get you murdered. For one thing, a sensible girl of unquestionable virtue did not go strolling on Sunset Avenue during the wee morning hours. A sensible girl who placed her trust in her fellowman knew she was stretching trust a bit too far when she went anywhere on the avenue after dark.

Hamilton could not believe she had been that stupid. Devotion to duty was fine, but that much devotion was ridiculous. His conclusions, then, from the morning's questionings were two. First, that the crime was committed at the social center, where she could reasonably have been during a late hour. And second, that Mary Blair had kept a few secrets from her co-workers.

Hamilton liked the second of his conclusions best. The only place that shining-example-of-young-womanhood line would take him was to a dead end. In all truth, he wanted to find some dirt in her life to work with. He was not interested in her many virtues; he was surprised that so many people could think of Mary Blair with so much approval. His reaction was, Aw, come on. She can't possibly be that good.

Maybe it was the heat.

Miss Kenton smiled at him from her chair and said, "Before we start, the rest of the girls would like to clean up the social center. It's a real mess after the dance and we usually clean it up during our lunch hour." She sat with her knees tightly together and her hands folded in her lap, while her body leaned forward slightly as though she was terribly interested in talking to a detective. "Some of us eat our lunches there too," she confided.

"I'm sorry about that," Hamilton said. "I would really like to be finished with that dance area. I would gladly tell them to clean it up. But I am the only cop here at the present time, and since I haven't been out of this office all morning, I

49

couldn't have checked that area yet, could I? I really would like to check it before you tidy up; if it doesn't interfere with lunch breaks and neatness too much."

"I'm sorry," she said. "Now I've made you angry."

"I'm not angry," Hamilton said. "I'm just doing the best I can, and I'd like a little cooperation." He picked up a sheet of paper from the desk and extended it toward her. "These are the names I have so far of the kids that might have been at the dance last night. Can you add any to the list?"

She read the list carefully and handed it back. "No," she said. "It was a neighborhood dance. There may have been other children present, but these were the regulars."

"How old would you say these kids are, on the average?"

She smiled at him. "Between twelve and sixteen."

That's a full-grown punk, he thought. He opened a thick envelope on the desk and pushed the list inside. "I've got the names and addresses of Miss Blair's cases here—you typed them for me, didn't you?"

"Yes."

"And Mary Blair would be the only one who would know anything about these cases that wasn't in the records, right?"

"Yes, that's right."

He pushed a paper clip onto the envelope and leaned back in the chair. "Fine," he said. "We'll check those out."

They watched each other silently for a long moment. "I haven't been able to learn anything about Miss Blair's personal life, Miss Kenton," he said finally. "Only about her job and such. It's sort of odd, don't you think?"

"Mary was one of our shy girls, Mr. Hamilton," she said. "You can't expect a girl like that to discuss her personal life over coffee like men."

50

"But the fact remains that someone must have been close to her. She doesn't have any relation here—no family at all?" He fingered the envelope. "It's been my experience that almost everyone will have a close friend to share their personal problems with. You might say that there is always someone who knows your business, no matter how shy you are."

"You've been a policeman for a long time, haven't you?" she asked.

"I didn't know it showed that much."

She smiled. She looked very wholesome and plain, and not trying to be a woman at all. Hamilton was impressed. "The girls," she added, inclining her head toward the other room. "They have the impression that you are cynical. I think you are just tired of people."

"Thanks for the five-minute analysis," he said. "I'm sorry I didn't have time to stop and pick up my book on etiquette before I came over. But we're talking about Mary Blair, and I don't have time to get analyzed."

"Mary always found time for everything, Mr. Hamilton. She liked people, all kinds of people."

"Somebody didn't like her," Hamilton said flatly. He was well aware of the fact that people became reluctant to answer his questions after a few minutes of his questioning. He had a lousy technique, he was told. Well, he knew all about the word-association technique, and the soft-hand technique. He used the Hamilton technique. He would ask simple questions, and expect simple answers. And he had better get the same answers when he asked those questions again. He did not see where liking or being tired of people had anything to do with it. He did not want to hear another biography on Mary Blair, the saint, either.

"I'm not going to tell you how wonderful Mary was," Miss Kenton said. "You've already heard that."

He watched her.

"I know because that's how she was, and you think that's odd. And you're wondering what she was like away from here, because being wonderful doesn't help you." She surprised Hamilton by lighting a cigarette before she said, "She was also a woman, with all the foolishness that we go through over men and love."

"Did you know her very well, Miss Kenton?"

She smiled. "Well enough to worry about her, with those foolish things like love, and if a girl should go to bed with a man because she wants to. Does that shock you, Mr. Hamilton? Does the job here cancel out the possibility that we might get the urge to go to bed with a man? Girls get laid every day in this city without the sanction of church, or a marriage certificate." She smiled. "Yes, I knew Mary well enough to talk over those things. I'm not quite the unimaginative spinster a welfare worker is supposed to be."

Hamilton considered her for a moment, then looked at his watch. It was eleven-thirty. "What time does this office go to lunch, Miss Kenton?"

"At twelve," she said. "But I can skip that if you think this will take longer. I could always go later."

"I was thinking that maybe I could check that social center now," Hamilton said. "And then I'd be finished here for now, except for our talk."

She waited, watching him.

"We could talk about this at lunch," he said. "Unless you . . ."

52

"I'd like to have lunch with you," she said, nodding. "I've never had lunch with a detective."

"It would save some time," he said as though apologizing. "I should get back to the station house as soon as possible."

"About Mary? Is that why you have to get back?"

He stood up behind the desk and made an attempt to tighten his tie. "In a way it's about her, just routine in a case like this," he said. "A pervert parade."

"I see," she said, not really seeing at all, and wondering if her reaction to him might be a form of opposites attracting. And she considered the chance that it could simply be a case of wondering how it would be to go to bed with him.

Lunch, at least, would be educational.

5

It is the tendency of police stations to run to extremes. They are either extremely dull and routine, or they are madhouses. You can be bored to death one minute, and wondering what part of the world fell on you the next.

It's a wonder that anybody wants a job that won't level off at either end of the extreme. It would be kind of nice to work at something where you knew what in hell was going to happen next. But then, if you worked at a job like that, you might never get the opportunity to get shot at in an alley, spit on in a riot, or kicked in the groin by a hopped-up hooker. And you wouldn't get the opportunity to take part in a pervert parade.

They were preparing a pervert parade at the East Bagley Street police station.

It was noon, and the station house was living up to its reputation as the hottest place in the city. The bullpen in the center of the cell block upstairs had been receiving a steady dribble of customers since the night's drunks had been unceremoniously liberated at eight that morning, without the usual breakfast of coffee and rolls, a breach of etiquette that a few of the regular sleep-ins had found rude enough to complain to the desk sergeant about. What the hell, if you're going to run that kind of jail, they'd get drunk over in the Fourth Ward, where a guy could depend on getting breakfast at least.

The desk sergeant assured them that things were tough all over, and booked them out. Then he removed his jacket in deference to the heat, and started booking in the prior sex offenders on a hold-for-questioning basis.

Between the drunks going and the sex offenders coming there had been a twelve-minute break. A quiet had settled on the building. And then they started bringing in the candidates for the pervert parade. The station house had not been quiet since.

There were twenty-five known sex offenders living in that area of the city which Lieutenant Kinsmiller was responsible for. That is, there were twenty-five after he had gone through the sex nut files, and had eliminated the nuts that he did not consider as necessary to list on the pickup sheets that Hamilton had requested. Overgeneralizing was another trying little trait of Hamilton's that Kinsmiller found irritating. And because Hamilton had requested the pick-up-and-hold, Kinsmiller had checked the request for just exactly whom the request had been directed at.

Hamilton had requested that the area's sex nuts be grabbed, period. The desk sergeant had interpreted this as all known sex offenders. It was a reasonable interpretation. Unfortunately, it covered too much ground. There were six file drawers in the records room that would come under that loose classification. Kinsmiller was not overjoyed by the possibility that Hamilton's request would have filled the station house with fairies, exhibitionists, and plain old window peepers, or dirty old men in general. He did not consider these as candidates for a pervert parade aimed at investigating a murder. He did consider rapes, assaults, and indecent assaults as true suspects, which would require checking immediately. Knowing Hamilton, he had checked the request and selected a priority list himself.

That goddamn Hamilton would have the entire precinct picked up and questioned every day if he could.

Kinsmiller's priority list had included twenty-five men with a hard sex rap on their records, and a memo for the working bulls to give second-choice interest to men with a record of incest charges, whom he called those who rolled their own. He had sent that list out and returned to his office with the satisfaction of knowing that Hamilton had not instigated a general harassment campaign.

He's using my station to make an ass out of me, Kinsmiller thought later. A deviate is a deviate to him. He would grab a fairy for this murder and grill him as quickly as a convicted rapist. That isn't rational. It isn't even practical procedure.

And if I question him about it?

Kinsmiller sighed. It would be Hamilton's pleasure to inform him that his request had been misunderstood. *He* certainly had not expected the desk sergeant to pass on a request that would create confusion and needless work for his fellow officers. The lieutenant didn't think that, did he? After all, he did know procedure, and wouldn't want to cause extra work or needless harassment for the sex nuts, just because they happen to have a file.

Kinsmiller slammed his hand down on his desk. That's exactly what that son-of-a-bitch would say too. He had to get that man out of his station!

He had known that for months, he remembered.

56

But how? Kinsmiller picked up the reports on his desk. He's solved some tough cases, he thought. When you shovel all this petty crap aside, he's solved some damn tough ones. Or did I put him on this one because I'd like to see him foul it up? It would give me the excuse I need to get him out of here. Jesus Christ! He's even got me questioning myself! I put him on this because he's the kind of cop that can do it. I know he's been screwing up a lot of little cases, but he'd been good before at a case like this. And Lord knows we're going to need this Blair thing solved. That poor kid.

Kinsmiller didn't like rape-os.

He tried not to let his dislike filter into his job, but he simply didn't like rape-os or potential rape-os. It was all very well and good to say that a rape-o is a psychological problem. And point out the fact that in the greatest percentage of rape cases the victim recovers both mentally and physically. You don't stop eating if you get force-fed once, do you? And you could toss in a few more facts like an estimated half of all rape cases are never reported, and in those that are, two out of three victims refuse to testify. With facts like that, you could get the idea that it can't be all that bad.

He still didn't like rape-os. The way he saw it was that sex was a pretty universal thing. And that any man who could walk, crawl, or fly down to Sunset Avenue could get his ashes hauled in any manner that fit his pocketbook. So he could not identify with the problem. There was just too much around to warrant stealing some.

But rapes kept on happening, no matter what his personal feelings were on the matter. And things like Mary Blair would happen to make rape show up in its ugliest form, and it became difficult to keep his personal feelings from sneaking into his unbiased duty.

Hamilton, he thought, was an example of a man who was able to perform his duty in an unbiased manner. Hamilton simply hated all punks impartially.

Kinsmiller glanced at his watch, and thought about the overcrowded bullpen on the second floor. It must be hot as hell up there waiting for a questioning, or deciding what lies to use to answer the questions with.

Lies were a necessity of life to Frankie Trumper. He was now deciding how many he could safely tell the cops. Maybe he should tell them the truth and get it over with. They always gave you that line about playing square with them and they'd play square with you. Yeah, Frankie thought. And when did you ever get a square deal from a cop?

Don't panic, he told himself. They don't have a thing on you. They could never figure out how it happened. They had been lucky on that first one. He would beat this one. It hadn't even been rape like they think; not really rape.

So the only one who had been square in this mess was Mary. Square was one of their favorite words, he mused.

He remembered the doctor out at the prison. Frankie, he'd said, we can't help you unless you play square with us. We can't cure a problem that we don't know about. So he'd figured what could he lose, and he'd talked. He'd gone into that office and he'd told the doc all about Frankie Trumper.

And you know what that silly son-of-a-bitch said? After asking all those stupid questions? He'd said, Frankie, part of your problem is that you hate women. That's the kind of crap you get from a square.

58

What kind of a stupid idea was that? Hate women? How can you hate them when you wanted to love them? He liked to feel them. He liked to watch them walk. How could he hate them when he liked them like that? He even liked the ones that didn't want to let him feel them. Of course, he didn't go around telling them he loved them; he'd only told one of the bitches that, and she'd made a fool out of him.

He shrugged. The loon doctor was a little crazy anyway. Anyone who talked to nuts all day had to be crazy himself. Frankie was glad that he hadn't seen him anymore after that hate-women crap. He never hated anything that nice. He got a little mad at them sometimes because they didn't want to be loved, but he didn't hate them. They were nice.

His hands were sweating.

Mary had been nice like that from the first, he remembered. He wiped his hands with the bottom of his shirt. It was hot and smoky as hell in the bullpen. He looked out through the bars and down the hall to the clock above the door. It was one o'clock.

He'd bet he got fired if he missed work again. It was a lousy job anyway. That was where it had all started. He'd met Mary Blair because of that lousy job. But he hadn't hated her then. Sure, he'd thought she was one of those high-class snobbish bitches, but he'd only wanted to teach her a lesson. He could tell she would be easy from the start.

But he hadn't hated her.

He lay on his bunk, feeling the hardness of iron under his body, and closed his eyes as he thought about his first meeting with Mary. It had been April then.

The city was bleeding gray into the gutters, oozing water

59

from the snow heaped in vacant lots and in the alleys. It had been raw and cold outside. He remembered the cold because he had been able to choose between a radio for his room or a coat; he had got the radio and was looking for a coat to steal as soon as he could find an unattended one.

He was not used to the chill wind as he shivered and walked the blocks between the hash house and the welfare building.

The lousy bitches could have brought the tray back, he thought as he walked. That's the kind of thanks you get from those goody-goody bitches. He couldn't see why they'd moved that lousy office down here anyway. They thought they were too good to sit in the hash house and drink their coffee.

So they talk the boss into a delivery service. For twenty lousy rolls and cookies, they want a catering service every day. And who's got to do the delivering? Him, the goddamn dishwasher, that's who. Man, this must be some sight to the creeps around here; they must really get their kicks seeing him carrying goodies to a social center.

That was another thing. Big deal—the Path; now the punks have a place where they can socialize, they say. Yeah, he'd like to see half the getting together those kids were doing when the chaperon wasn't around. He'd heard that there was more screwing going on in the locker room than there was dancing being done in the gym.

To hell with it. He didn't care if that bunch started holding prayer meetings on the corner. He just didn't like walking two blocks every day to bring them coffee.

The least they could do was bring the tray back. One of the girls will drop it off after work, they'd said. So where the hell is it? Maybe they figure that he could start coming down and getting it too, after a month of playing waiter for them.

Lousy uptown bitches. He'd like to shake them up; get in there when they're all sitting around like they usually are when he comes in, and tell them who their delivery boy is. Get ready, girls, he could say. I just finished doing four years for rape, and I'm thinking of running up the score. He'd bet they would clamp their hands over their box behind that. He smiled at the thought.

Hell, they might figure that it would be their one chance to get laid, and rape *him*. They were probably like the rest, yelling no all the time they were trying to help you get their pants off.

He could tell that Mary was ripe to have them taken off, when he walked into the place and asked for the tray. She stopped pinning up party decorations and looked at him steadily, like she was thinking of buying him for lunch break.

"I can't bring over the coffee until I get the tray," he said. "The boss only got that one."

"Oh," she said, and put her hand up to her mouth. "It was my turn to bring it back. I forgot; I'm sorry."

"Yeah," Frankie said. "Can I have it?"

She was attractive in a mousy sort of way. Not much makeup, and clothes that hardly let you know she had a nice set of knockers. The mousy type were always easy to make on the avenue, he remembered. They only had one thing to offer, so it didn't take them long to get their legs up in the air, if they wanted a guy to stick around.

"Of course," she said. "I'm sorry that you had to walk all the way over here in this cold. It's cold out, isn't it?"

Frankie shrugged. "I'll live, I guess."

She kept standing there, watching him and smiling. "Do you ever come down here to use the gym?"

"No," he said. "I only bring the coffee. Why?"

She flushed slightly. "You have an excellent natural build. I thought perhaps . . . "

No, he thought. I got that from lifting weights out at the state prison. "I exercise in my room," he said. "Like to keep in shape, you know."

"I'll get that tray," she said.

He watched her walk as she crossed the room. She had a nice walk; nothing spectacular, but nice enough. Wide hips for a good ride, and nice legs. Not bad for a mouse. Too bad she didn't put on some makeup and a tight skirt. She'd probably look all right. A guy might make a pass at her then, if she acted like she'd deliver.

The thought had come to him suddenly. Why not? She couldn't be having any more fun than a mouse on the avenue. The uptown cats didn't want to take out a plain Jane either.

He watched her search for the tray across the room. Think they're too good to sit in the hash house, huh? Too good to mix with the people around here, with their clean-living crap and innocent act.

He decided then that he was going to lay her. He was going to take the uptown bitch and make her like it. He smiled. And it wouldn't be rape either. He wasn't about to give that parole agent an excuse to send him back. But there were other ways. He remembered the trick that an old gigolo had told him about in the pen. It would work on a stupid mouse like this one. She'd never know she'd been had like a wised-up

62

chick from the avenue would. Yeah, he'd fix it so she didn't think she was too good to give out a little.

It would be a kick, laying a social worker. He watched her with a hot eagerness growing in him. He'd like it better if he could just take her. He would be just taking her, in a way. The thought made him feel good. But he had to get next to her first. He had to play with her, get her to like him.

It wouldn't be such a bad idea at that. Maybe if he played with her, he wouldn't be trying to prong that girl at the rooming house. He was worried about that. He was watching that bitch too much. Even if she was a tramp, he wasn't thinking of buying any; he was always thinking of taking it. He was watching her too much. Horny like he was, he could get into trouble.

Playing around with this mouse would be better. And he didn't think he'd have to rape her either. He was going to be careful though, in case something did happen. In case that old gigolo had been wrong about it working.

She'd probably like it, he thought as he watched her start back toward him with the tray.

He had wanted her to like it, he thought now as he lay on his bunk in the bullpen. Hell, he'd known she was a bitch even then, the way she'd smiled at him and talked about his build.

He should tell the cops about that. He should tell them how she acted, but he'd liked her anyway. He wouldn't have gone through all that trouble getting to know her if he'd hated her, would he? He went through a lot of trouble so he wouldn't hurt her. They couldn't call that rape. He'd never asked the gigolo about that.

He could tell the cops about the coffee anyway. That would explain how he knew her, working right there on University like that.

But . . .

Well, what about Rawls? That pious bastard might violate him just for knowing her, with his rap. He might send him back even if they couldn't prove anything. He'd have to lie, and stick to just seeing her around.

Frankie pulled his handkerchief from his pocket and scrubbed his face. He had to get his story straight! And stick with it!

But if someone had seen him, and remembered. What then? They'd throw the book at him then. He wiped his face again.

He'd be all right if he had a good lawyer, he thought. So the cops couldn't trick him into admitting anything. But even if he could afford a lawyer, the cops would think for sure he'd done it if he yelled for one now. He wasn't even charged with anything yet. He had to think up an excuse.

He thought about Mr. Rawls.

He sat up on the bunk. Yeah, Mr. Clean himself. He'd help. I want to help you, Frankie, he always said. And he was a chump. Rawls might believe him, and with Rawls there the cops would be careful. He knew his rights. He didn't have to say a word if he got someone to help him.

Frankie swung his legs off the bunk and sat up. He walked across the bullpen, past the two tables where the other men were playing cards, and stopped at the bars where he could see the trusty sitting on a chair in the corridor.

"Trusty," he said. "Hey, trusty."

The man looked up. "Yeah?"

64

"I want to make a phone call," Frankie said, smiling. "I'm allowed one call, ain't I? That's the law."

"So make it," the man said, grinning. "You should have made it downstairs."

"How about making one for me?"

"I ain't got time," the man said, stretching.

Frankie felt his pockets. "I'll give you a buck," he said.

The trusty grinned again. "A buck won't buy you the right time of day. I ain't supposed to make calls for you creeps, you know."

"Two," Frankie said, pulling the folded bills from his pocket. "That's all I got."

The trusty took the bills and tucked them into his pocket. "Who do you want called? Your stockbroker?"

"My parole agent," Frankie said.

The man stared at him and shrugged. "It's your money, Mack," he said. "What's the bastard's name?" He paused. "What do you want him for anyway? You freaks got enough trouble with the dicks that are going to be coming up here. They got one that's a real son-of-a-bitch in the cop-out room."

"That's why I want my parole agent," Frankie said. "I don't want any bum rap on this beef."

"Yeah," the trusty said. "I know all about it; you didn't do it. I've heard the story before."

He stood there grinning and waited for the name.

When Hamilton left Miss Kenton after lunch, he had listened to what he considered a sad story. Any story about young love was a pretty sad story as far as he was concerned. He had always considered love as a misunderstanding between two fools. Or a misunderstanding on one fool's part and tolerance for it on the other's. There always seemed to be a lot of misery connected with it.

Mary Blair's love life meant misery for Hamilton, because now he had to find out who the man was she'd been dating. She had confided to Miss Kenton that he was a jewel in the rough.

Jewel he might be, Hamilton observed. But he was none too eager to come down to the station house and confide his relationship with the girl to the police. There was something fishy about a steady relationship with a man whom the girl had never named for some reason. Miss Kenton's opinion was that Mary Blair had a lover. It was also her opinion that she was having some difficulties with her lover. Not that Mary had confided that; it was only an opinion.

Hamilton could think of quite a few difficulties that a social worker might have with a lover. Hamilton had a dirty mind anyway. He considered the possibility that Mary Blair had not been putting out in traditional lover fashion, and her lover had got tired of that sort of courtship, and taken some. He could build up a pretty good possible motive on that. He forces her, then panics because she threatens to yell rape. And one dead body results.

Fine, Hamilton thought. So just who was that lover? There was motive enough for him to be a suspect. Half the goddamn city seemed to be suspects. He could just as well dig out a phone directory and start with the A's. It was just too bad that they didn't put out a directory on punks and potential punks. You could bet that the killer would be listed in that. He was probably down in the bullpen right now.

Hamilton sat in his car and studied his notebook. There were a number of items he had listed as needing attention. At the top of the page he had written two words:

"Pervert Parade."

Next: "Punks who attended dance."

And: "Check Miss Blair's personal effects for key to social center."

He had also reminded himself to: "Put the stoolies on checking moll-buzzers."

There was another notation suggesting that it was going to be a job checking out the DCA cases, and additional notes reminded him to: get a court order prior to a visit to her room, pick up lab report and autopsy, check Mr. Grewe's alibi. And now he wrote the word: "Lover." He stared at it, and crossed it out and wrote: "Check for address book, personal letters from male friends."

He studied the notes and sighed. Now that's what he called an open case. He fitted the pen into the wire binding of the notebook. It was more information than he'd expected this early in the case. But it wasn't saying anything. Punks, mysterious lovers, rape-os. How the hell do normal lives get so complicated when you dig into them?

He started his car and edged into the traffic lane, ignoring the honking horns. Maybe the lab report would narrow it down for him.

And questioning the rape-os would narrow it down some more. He smiled at the thought. There was nothing like a good questioning. He liked to see a rape-o sweat. He clenched his hands tightly against the wheel as he drove.

He wondered if that bastard Kinsmiller was enjoying the pervert parade he'd ordered. It wasn't just Kinsmiller riding him like he was a rookie, he thought. He'd seen enough skippers at the station to know what the lieutenant was trying to do with his petty harassment, like giving him the case when it wasn't his. The whole force was like that, weeding out the old cops and bringing in those candy-ass cops with fancy educations. Kinsmiller wanted him busted out, and that would be it for him. He wouldn't last a month at a desk job, not after being a Bagley Street bull for all those years.

He didn't know how to do anything else. The thought surprised him. Anyway, he was a good cop. He'd just been making some mistakes lately. But it wasn't his fault that the arrests didn't stick like they used to. He couldn't lose another one, or Kinsmiller would have what he needed to boot him out. He had to get a case against this killer, or lose everything he'd worked for.

He had that twisted-gut feeling about this one. It was going to be one of those cases he'd wrap for them, and some idiot judge would put the bastard back on the street to do it again. It wasn't like that twenty years ago; a cop had a chance then.

He stopped at a traffic light and rolled the window down, while he watched two T-shirted locals leaning against the front of the pool hall.

Punks, he thought. The lousy city's full of punks.

There was only one way to cure a punk. It made him feel better to think about that. If it happened like that it would be a solved case. No writ or appeal ever got a punk out of a grave.

Nothing would get the girl out of one, would it?

When he parked his car down the street from the police station, Rawls wondered what there was about a precinct house that he didn't like.

The precinct houses were the sifting pots, where the evidence and the crimes were picked apart and reshaped in a way that could well decide the impartiality and the degree of justice that would come later.

There was nothing dignified about a precinct house. The East Bagley Street station was a soot-covered structure that seemed to squat impassively in the sun's glare. There were bars on all of the windows, except for the street side of the first floor, and there was two-inch steel screen behind the bars. The frosted-glass windows behind the screen were open to the breezeless street.

He had not visited this particular station before. He did not like visiting police stations, because a visit usually meant that he had not been able to reach one of his cases, but the law had.

It was also his first visit to a precinct house at the direct request of a parolee. He told them all the same thing. Call me. That's what a parole agent is for. If you have trouble, call me. Nobody had called before but the police.

And now it seemed that one man had believed him. He

69

had been asked for help. That is maybe not an impressive score for seven months in the job, but he kept his word, he was ready to help. If all of his cases had called, he would have been ready to help. It was all very simple to Rawls. It was his job to help people. He had accepted that as what he considered right for him to do.

He had read the file on Frankie Trumper during his lunch hour. And though he might agree with Cochan that justice was a fickle bitch, he had found nothing in the file to make him change his opinion about the man's parole. He was guilty of nothing but being picked up for questioning by the police.

Rawls went up the steps and through the building's open doors. It was hot inside too, and it smelled strongly of disinfectant. There was no way to get around it, he simply didn't like police stations. There was an air of fresh crime and raw fear about them. He was thankful that he had not decided to become a police officer, a job in which he would have had to deal with crime in the most basic mixture. It was easier dealt with after justice and time had taken the rawness out of it. Rape, for example, was simply a word for a past offense when it was found in a man's file. He did not see it during the hours after it had occurred. It was therefore no more than a four-letter word for an offense that it was part of his job to keep from recurring. Prevention of repeat offenses was the job he understood well, he thought. But he still disliked the basicness of a station house. Justice at a basic point could be anything but that.

The booking desk was to the right of the doors as he entered. A uniformed patrolman stood in front of the desk with a dark-haired girl. She was handcuffed to his left wrist. The

70

sergeant was staring at them and shaking his head. He was asking the patrolman, "She was doing *what* in the park?"

The patrolman's face was red. "She was exposing herself, Sarge."

"How was that?"

"She was lying on a blanket just off the path, reading a book." He glanced at the girl. "On her back."

The sergeant looked at the blouse and skirt the girl was wearing. "She was lying on her back, huh? So?"

"With her legs up," the patrolman said.

"So?"

"She hasn't got any pants on, Sarge. She was exposing herself."

"He's never seen one before," the girl said gaily. "It scared him to death."

"Shut up," the patrolman said. He looked at the sergeant. "Well?"

"Was there a crowd enjoying the view?"

"Just him and the squirrels," the girl said. "I'll bet he made fifty trips past there." She giggled.

"How old are you?" the sergeant asked.

"Seventeen."

"You like to run around the park showing your bottom?"

"He was the only one looking," the girl said. "Nobody else noticed. He's a sex fiend or something, I'll bet."

"Sarge," the patrolman said desperately. "I was by there twice. The second time I went over and told her that she was showing everything she had."

"Not quite," the girl said.

"So what happened?"

71

"She told me not to knock a good thing. She wasn't charging for the show."

"Now he knows what one looks like," the girl said. She held up the arm with the handcuff on it. "See, he didn't want me to get away from him when he found out."

"You want to take that into court?" the sergeant asked. "She had her legs up, and you happened to notice?" He grinned.

"He noticed a lot," the girl said.

"Ah . . . hell, Sarge." The patrolman stopped, undecided.

"Get her to hell out of here," the sergeant said. "You see her at it again and we'll turn her over to the vice squad. See how she likes a VD check on her record."

"Hey!" the girl said. "I was only kidding. I just thought I'd have some fun with him."

"Don't have fun at our cops' expense," the sergeant warned.

The patrolman started off, dragging the girl. He stopped, looking at the handcuffs. "What am I supposed to do with her?" he wanted to know.

"Take her back to the park. Take her out and buy her some pants. I don't care. Just get her out of here."

The girl was smiling at the patrolman as the sergeant watched them go out through the doors. Then he leaned back in his chair and said, "These rookies," to no one in particular and burst out laughing. Abruptly, as though Rawls had suddenly intruded on his cheerful mood, he asked, "What's your problem, mister?"

"I'm Chuck Rawls, Sergeant," he said. "I'd like to see Frankie Trumper. I'm his parole agent."

It was not that Lieutenant Kinsmiller had anything against parole agents. They were fine, dedicated men in the city's correctional department. He was sure too that parole agents did their jobs as competently as cops did. It wasn't that he had anything against them at all.

So why wasn't this one out trying to rehabilitate someone instead of at his station house? They had a working agreement with parole agents. The police would tend to crime, parole agents to supervision. And if it should appear that rehabilitation had not taken effect, and a charge was placed against a parolee, the police would notify the parole agent to that effect. *Then* the agent could be expected to come down to the station house; there was a reason to come down. The usual procedure was for them to stay the hell out of the station until due process of law decided if there was reason to violate or not violate a man's parole.

It was a sound working agreement. It was an agreement which served to lessen the confusion around the station house when there was a lineup or a pervert parade. He didn't need a few dozen parole agents showing up to ask how things were going, as if they were worried about a failure in their program.

It was bad enough when attorneys dropped by for a simple questioning. He was only trying to eliminate possible suspects with a few questions and as quickly as possible. He did not need attorneys, parole agents, or the society of sob sisters descending on his station house to question his procedure.

He ran a good station house. All you had to do was take a look around. There wasn't a rubber hose in the place. There were no facilities for giving superhot enemas, nor any ammonia

73

sponges in the interrogation rooms. His detectives didn't even carry their blackjacks in there.

Kinsmiller damn well resented the fact that some parole agent should show up because he was running a routine, every-day-type questioning. He did not know everything that went on in his station, of course, but you could bet that he knew how to handle a questioning properly.

So why did this parole agent want to disrupt normal procedure and see his parolee before he'd even been charged with anything? It was a goddamn imposition and, coming from a man who should know better, it was an obvious breach of unwritten policy.

It bothered Kinsmiller.

And it bothered him especially because Hamilton was one of the three detectives upstairs holding the pervert parade. He did not like the idea of an outsider attending any questioning that Hamilton was involved in. Listening to Hamilton question a sex offender was like getting a verbal description of the history of the sexual sins of man.

So Kinsmiller, who insisted that all questionings be kept within the legal boundaries of the courts and rules of interrogation, and who would have personally suspended any man who broke them, was more or less reluctant to determine whether Hamilton's verbal tactics would fit into the boundaries of a parole agent who might not be reasonable enough to follow a policy that had worked effectively for years. Hamilton could be a pain in the ass without trying to be.

Kinsmiller wondered what this parole agent was trying to be besides a pain and a disrupter of procedure. A set procedure and enforcing rules were two of his greatest aids in running the station, even at the routine level of a questioning for a murder suspect.

The desk sergeant had informed him that Rawls was waiting at the booking desk. Kinsmiller had considered his request. The rules by which he could measure the request were simple. Attorneys were permitted to visit their clients at any time. Family and clergy were also admitted during the posted visiting hours. There were no provisions in the rules for parole agents. His course then could be determined by the catchall rule that permission for visits of an unlisted nature will be at the discretion of the officer in charge.

He could rightly exercise that privilege and flatly say no to Rawls because his visit would disrupt procedure. But Kinsmiller was a reasonable man. He did not like it, but he would attempt to acquaint Rawls with the purpose of the helpful unwritten agreement between parole agents and the police.

He asked the desk sergeant to send Rawls in.

"Why do you want to see Trumper?" he asked. "We haven't charged him with anything. Couldn't it wait until we're finished?"

"Frankie said he would like to talk to me," Rawls said. "I don't know why, but I suppose he's worried about being violated. I would like to tell him that if he's clean, he's safe."

"He's been picked up before; he knows how safe he is," Kinsmiller said. "So why can't this wait?"

"I would like the man to know that he's got somebody on his side as long as he's innocent. I'd like him to know that a parole agent is not just a fancy name for a guard."

"We'll tell him you were here," Kinsmiller said. "That should give him all of the moral support he needs to answer a few questions. This is just a routine pickup—not worth the time it took you to drive down here."

"I think it is, Lieutenant. Maybe he's finding out that I'm on his side as I've been telling him. If a few minutes' visit will prove that to him, I don't think it's wasted time."

"I think it's wasted time—our time. Listen. I've got twenty-five men up there to question, and only three detectives to do it with. Do you think I can give one of them a visit from you people without every one of them starting to yell for their parole agents as well as their lawyers? This is a routine process. I'm not going to start giving them ideas. We'll call you if we find anything to hold him on." He paused. "That's the usual procedure. Besides, what you're asking will put my men at a disadvantage."

"I don't see how it—"

"Do you want me to give you a lesson in police interrogation?" Kinsmiller asked. "If I didn't think that the police and you people were on the same side, I'd tell you to go to hell. You *are* against crime, aren't you?"

"Lieutenant . . ."

"All right. Forget I said that." Kinsmiller smiled. "Try to see it my way. This is a routine questioning, right?"

"Yes."

"What we're trying to do is like shooting in the dark; we need everything we can get on our side." Rawls nodded, and the lieutenant went on. "First, we try to get a psychological advantage by pulling them all in here and making them wait. They know what they're here for, and they worry about it. They establish their alibis in their minds, and remember exactly where they were last night. They will have their answers ready when they hit the interrogation rooms. The ones who are telling the truth will be worried, but they will be sure of their alibis. If any of them are lying they will have enough time to think up a fancy story, and they will make mistakes with it, and the more they worry, the more mistakes they'll make." He grinned at Rawls. "This is my theory of interrogations of this sort. If I let you go up there to see Trumper, it might give him the support he needs to lie and not make any mistakes. I'd be working against myself, wouldn't I?"

Rawls thought about it. Then he smiled and said, "I still want to see Trumper, Lieutenant. Did you ever consider the possibility that he might want to tell me something he wouldn't tell your men? He might have something he wants to get off his chest."

Kinsmiller sighed wearily. "It's a waste of time," he said, "but you can hear his sad story after he's been interrogated. I can't give *any* of them a break."

Upstairs, Hamilton wasn't interested in giving any of the sex nuts a break. He was questioning the fifth man he'd called in since he'd got back from lunch. There was no fun at all in a pervert parade when the questioning had to be done at the station.

The objective of all three detectives doing the interrogation in separate rooms upstairs was to narrow down the number of men on the pervert parade to a few finalists who would be treated to a more detailed questioning, and further narrowing down. There was a lot of work involved in a pervert parade when you knew that it was quite possible that you could eliminate suspects until there were no longer any of the original pervert parade left. Then all you had for your efforts were

77

some still unanswered questions and the distinct feeling that you'd been lied to. Nobody had fun at a pervert parade.

It had the same dullness as a standard lineup. It was strictly the routine business of ushering men from the bullpen to one of the three interrogation rooms down the hall and going through a familiar routine.

The interrogation rooms were small and devoid of comfort. And being alone in a small gray room with a serious-looking detective had a way of making suspects uneasy. Especially if they were in the room with Hamilton. To ensure that the suspect was not at all at ease with his surroundings, Hamilton would first read aloud his record. And after he had reminded the suspect of the act that he had offended society with before, he would ask what he had been doing last night.

You were likely to get a lot of wise-ass answers with a system like that.

By the time Hamilton began questioning Frankie Trumper, he was hoping that this one had come into the room with a confession in his pocket and repentance in his heart.

Frankie sat on the room's single wooden chair and watched Hamilton read the file on his desk.

It was very quiet in the room until Hamilton looked up and said, "How's being a rape-o these days, Frankie? Finding that it's keeping you busy coming down here?"

"I didn't come down," Frankie said. "I was brought."

"Well, you can't expect not to be asked questions once in a while when you spend your time running around the neighborhood with nothing else but a camel-hair overcoat and a hard-on."

Frankie wet his lips. "I had all my clothes on that night. That was years ago."

"I thought you were the one who did that," Hamilton

78

said. "We had one rape-o here who used to wear a jockstrap and a football helmet." He grinned. "Had a hell of a time getting a make on him—that's all the women could remember was that football helmet. I thought you were the camel-hair overcoat one who liked young girls."

"Why don't you let it alone, man," Frankie said. "I did my time. I'm clean, see. Why keep bringing it up? Can't a guy go straight after one mistake around here?"

"But you're not quite straight, Frankie. We don't quite trust you yet. That's why you're on parole. We bring you in here to keep you straight."

"Yeah," Frankie said. "Sure, man. I know why you bring me down here."

Hamilton smiled and stood up, coming around the desk casually. "The name is Detective Hamilton to you, punk," he said.

"Sure, man."

Hamilton slapped him across the mouth. "Detective Hamilton," he repeated.

"Pardon me all to hell, Mister Detective Hamilton," Frankie said. "What's with you anyway?"

Hamilton slapped him again. "Detective Hamilton, punk," he said. "You get wise with me and I'll blackjack you till you piss all over yourself." He closed his hand into a fist.

"Detective Hamilton," Frankie said quickly.

Hamilton went back around the desk and sat down. "You learn fast, Frankie. I like punks who learn fast. You just keep learning and be cooperative."

"I'm always cooperative," Frankie said. "You ask the questions and I'll answer them." He waited a moment. "I came down voluntarily with the cop, didn't I?"

"Sure you did."

"Sure, and you know why? 'Cause I know my rights. I don't have to answer any questions unless I want to. Aren't you going to give me the lecture on my constitutional rights first?"

"There's only one thing I hate worse than a jailhouse lawyer," Hamilton said.

"Yeah?"

"And that's a wise-ass jailhouse lawyer," Hamilton stated, and rubbed his hands together. "Are you going to be a wise-ass, Frankie?"

Frankie wiped his hands on his shirt front. "Ask your questions," he said. "I'm clean. I had nothing to do with this murder."

"How do you know we want to ask questions about that?"

"What else would it be?"

"You been getting laid pretty regular, Frankie?"

"What the hell is that for? I don't have to answer that."

"Know Mary Blair?"

"Yeah. I seen her around. At least I think it was her."

"You *do* know Mary Blair?"

"She came in the place I work for coffee once in a while. The boss mentioned her name, I guess. I don't remember where I heard it."

"Remember," Hamilton advised.

"I knew her when she came in for coffee, that's all."

"What did she do, wear a sign saying 'I'm Mary Blair'? How'd you know her, Frankie?"

"Someone mentioned her name. How'd I know a lousy welfare worker anyway?"

"What were you doing last night?"

"When last night? I work nights."

80

"From when to when?"

"Three in the afternoon until nine at night."

"What did you do after work?"

"I went home and went to bed."

"At nine o'clock!"

"Damn right," Frankie said. "You ever wash dishes in a hash house from three to nine, six hours straight? I went home and went to bed. I was tired."

"You went to bed right away? Right home and right to bed?"

"I was in bed by ten anyway."

"Who saw you? You talk to anybody around your place?"

"How do I know who saw me? I'm on parole, see, I got to be in my place by eleven anyway. Besides, I'm damn glad to get to bed by ten."

"No witnesses, huh?"

"You charging me with something?"

"Not yet."

"So I don't need witnesses then."

Hamilton pointed a thick finger at Frankie. "You," he said slowly, "need witnesses, punk. You're a sex freak on parole, and don't tell me what you need."

"How about *you?*" Frankie said. "Have you got a witness that says I wasn't in bed? I ain't been charged. What do I have to prove?"

"Prove to me that you were in bed last night after ten. Prove you weren't out running around with a camel-hair overcoat and a hard-on."

"I told you where I was."

"How long you been watching the Blair girl?"

"I didn't watch Mary—I wasn't watching her."

81

"How's that? You didn't watch who?"

"That welfare worker."

"Why'd you call her Mary? You know her well enough to use her first name, punk?"

"I didn't know her. I seen her around."

"You knew her all right."

"How are you going to prove that, cop? Listen, to hell with this crap. I want a lawyer. I want my parole agent. You people ain't pinning any beef like this on me. I know my rights."

"Rights!" Hamilton said as he came around the desk and stood in front of Frankie. "You goddamn animal! You rape-o son-of-a-bitch. I remember the first girl you raped! Don't talk to me about your rights, punk!"

"I ain't talking to you at all," Frankie said, sweating.

Hamilton opened his hand. "I love you wise punks," he said. "You're the kind that like it down here." He waited. "I'm going to get you booked on suspicion of murder, punk."

Frankie was silent.

"And rape," Hamilton added. "We're going to get to know each other real good. I'm going to spend some time with you."

Frankie had nothing to say. He sat still and sweated, and then he looked at Hamilton and asked, "Who was the guy that made the scene with the football helmet and jockstrap?"

It was near 4 P.M. before the questioning session was over.

Rawls had waited.

Sitting on the gray bench near the booking desk, he

82

watched the routine running of the police station with impatient eyes. He had argued a point with the lieutenant because he felt he was doing the right thing. He had won his point. He could not very well go back to his office, because he had to wait.

You didn't change your mind about helping people over a small thing like not being able to help them instantly. Still, the lieutenant could have let him see Frankie for a few minutes during the questioning.

All he wanted to prove was that parole agents were willing to help their men. Those that were trying to go straight anyway. To prove that, he was sitting on a hard bench in a hot room. You had to start somewhere, he guessed. He guessed that this was as good a place as any. It was probably better than most places. Frankie was being shown distrust and suspicion here. It was a perfect place to show some understanding and faith in him. To show him that he had nothing to fear unless he had committed the crime.

Was Frankie innocent?

He hadn't thought of that. That was for the courts to decide. And until they did, he had to show some faith in the man's innocence. You had to understand the man's problem. You had to keep him from getting the attitude "What the hell, I might just as well do it if everybody thinks I did."

When they started thinking like that, they were on their way back. He could not afford to doubt a man's innocence until his guilt was proved. An agent needed a large dose of faith.

He waited. He watched the men come down the stairs as the afternoon wore on. They came in twos and threes and always with a detective, who would take them to the booking desk and sort through the personal property envelopes until he found the property of the men being released.

The envelopes were in a temporary wire rack near the desk sergeant's chair. Rawls had watched the rack empty slowly, until there was only one envelope remaining. He had watched the three detectives come down the stairs alone and enter the lieutenant's office. Frankie had not followed the pattern and claimed his envelope with cheerful relief.

Rawls wondered why Frankie was receiving additional attention. He smiled wryly, reflecting that he had somehow expected that. Why else had the man asked for help? Of course he had expected trouble clearing himself, or he wouldn't have wanted to explain it to a parole agent. He probably wanted to explain some simple circumstances that he was worried might get him violated.

Circumstances couldn't get him violated, Rawls thought. He hoped that there was no more to the matter than that. The man was doing fine on parole, according to the record. He had to have faith in that record; it was all he had.

He watched the door to the lieutenant's office open and Kinsmiller start toward him.

"You can see Trumper now," he said as he approached.

Rawls smiled. "Has he been questioned?"

"Sure," Kinsmiller said. "You can pat him on the back or do anything you want to for his morale."

"Just my job." Rawls stopped. He stared at Kinsmiller and frowned. "Is he in trouble?"

"Well, that depends on how you look at it. We're going to investigate his story. . . . We're booking him on suspicion."

84

He watched Rawls for a long time, and added, "Do you still want to see him?"

"Yes," Rawls said. "It doesn't change anything. He still needs someone on his side."

"And that's you, huh, Rawls?" Kinsmiller asked. "Why?"

Rawls mustered up a smile. "Why not?" he asked. "He's one of my men."

Kinsmiller chewed the end of his pipestem. "I think I'd worry about the ones worth saving."

"That's exactly what I'm doing, Lieutenant," Rawls said. "I haven't met any of the other kind yet."

Kinsmiller nodded at the sergeant at the desk. "Call upstairs," he said. "Tell the turnkey to let Mr. Rawls see Trumper. He wants to listen to a sad story." He nodded and turned away from Rawls.

Rawls stood and watched the lieutenant's retreating back. He felt suddenly alone in an alien place; there was a sense of being a tolerated intruder. He had aligned himself against the station's function. He had become a part of the enemy camp, a man to be treated with bare civility and without any special consideration. And all he had wanted was to remain unbiased.

He was the buffer between his cases and society, and it would be nice if he could remain neutrally between the police and the courts too, a position from which he might salvage a man. It was an uneasy neutrality at best.

He turned and walked toward the stairs leading up to the cell block.

7

September 16 was a Saturday, a day of rest for many of the city's heat-tested citizens. It was a day to go to the beach or just sit on the front steps and sweat, or a day to find an air-conditioned bar where you could nurse a beer and be thankful that Monday was still more than a full day away.

You could do a lot of things on Saturday.

Frankie Trumper lay on his bunk in his cell and scratched his crotch. He thought that he probably had a dose of crabs again. The cell must have had a million of them just waiting for him.

He always seemed to develop a dose of crabs in jail. They could fumigate the cell, shower and blue-ointment him, and supply laundry-fresh bedding. It never helped. He still got the crabs. He was no longer surprised by their mysterious appearance. He would, instead, inspect the inhabited areas of his body with purposeful intent, and capture the tiny vermin with all the gentleness he could manage. He would then carry his captive to the door of his cell and drop it on the flat steel plate under the opening where his tray was passed during mealtimes. With this accomplished, he would call the guard on duty to the door and proceed to expand the crab's feeding area by blowing it from the steel plate onto the guard's uniform. He

86

did not want the guard to miss the opportunity of having to solve the problem of where a dose of crabs came from.

He had not considered that activity as a pastime yet on Saturday morning, and was content to scratch and hope that the itching he had developed overnight was a matter of imagination. He was concerned with more pressing matters, like the possibility of a murder charge.

But it was only suspicion of murder, he thought. Rawls had told him that. Booked on suspicion of murder, he had said. There was nothing to worry about. They couldn't tie him in.

They couldn't get a grand jury indictment on his just knowing her. He couldn't tell them any more than that now. Rawls had believed him, hadn't he? He'd promised to get him an attorney; he must have believed him.

Frankie reached up and touched his lips. The swelling had gone down. That was a good idea, he thought. Rawls had been a sucker for it. All he'd done was dab at his mouth with his handerkerchief while they were talking.

He'd bet Rawls was screaming police brutality all over city hall. Frankie grinned. That lousy Hamilton hadn't slapped him hard enough though. He'd had to bite the inside of his lip to make it start bleeding before Rawls came up to see him.

He felt the inside of his lip with his tongue. It was a little sore, he noticed. But it sure had been worth it.

Level with me, Frankie, Rawls had said. Well, he'd leveled with him all right. That stupid bastard had almost drooled with sympathy. Man, he'd even said that he'd see they didn't question him again without a lawyer.

Frankie folded his hands behind his head and stared at the light above his head. He had it made on this one, he assured himself. An attorney wouldn't let him say a thing. And now that he'd been booked on suspicion, the bulls had only two more days to charge him with a beef or let him go.

That son-of-a-bitch Hamilton couldn't dig up a thing in two days. He'd been too careful. There wasn't a thing they could use to take to the DA and expect him to get an indictment on it. Even that stupid Hamilton wouldn't try that on his just knowing her.

They'd have to let him go, and he'd stick with the girls on the avenue; no more uptown bitches after this. He'd of been better off trying to prong that one at the rooming house. He could get hot just thinking about how that bitch walked. Maybe he could get to her the same way he'd got to Mary. Maybe . . .

What are you doing? They're trying to get you for murder, and you're thinking of a lay. But . . . Well, hell, there was nothing to sweat on this. Even his parole agent was on his side. Man, old Rawls really was a square cat. Frankie thought about it in amazement. He really believes the crap he spouts at you. That cat would go against his own mother if he thought she was wrong.

As long as you're clean, Frankie, he'd said.

He was as clean as a monk's sheet. He hadn't made any slips.

Frankie got up off the bunk and walked to the front of his cell. The clock on the wall in the corridor told him that it was almost nine o'clock. It was getting hot in the cell already, he noticed. He wondered if Rawls would get him that lawyer this morning. No matter; all he had to do now was keep his mouth shut. They wouldn't have enough to even interest the DA. It would be just his luck to have the papers play this up big though; his being on parole. Rawls would get a lot of heat then. He wondered how much heat that pious, upright bastard would take before he violated him just to show what a civil-minded servant he was.

He couldn't think like that, Frankie told himself. He hadn't made any mistakes. That is, nothing that Hamilton could find. He should be thinking that over. Real careful like, so he'd know just where the weak parts were in this.

He went back to his bunk.

He was beginning to feel uneasy, knowing Hamilton was out there digging. He guessed that even that moron wouldn't try to make something out of his calling her Mary. He guessed that nobody in the whole city would think that an ex-con and a welfare worker would have anything to do with each other.

When he'd decided to lay her, he'd been smart enough not to tell her he was an ex-con, he remembered. He'd decided on that after their first date. Some date! He had wanted to test her out on that one. To see how long it would take to get in her pants. He'd known she would have to trust him for it to work. He hadn't even got a feel of her that first date.

They went to a movie.

He hadn't gone to a movie in years. Frankie tried to remember if he'd made any mistakes for Hamilton to find that night. He had talked her into a drink after the movie. It was important to know if she drank for what he planned. He wanted her to be able to blame it on that if it worked.

She had sat and drunk a Tom Collins while she talked about her work as though she liked it.

"What do you get out of working in this neighborhood?" he asked. "Why work around here if you don't have to?" He felt a resentment for her enthusiasm.

89

"I talked about it too much," she said. "You're probably bored with listening to that already."

"Go ahead," he said. "I'm interested in finding out what makes you tick. I want to know all about you."

"You didn't expect me to go out with you tonight, did you?" she asked suddenly.

"I wasn't sure."

"Why was that?"

"I live around here, you just come down to work . . ." He let it trail off. "I'm not in your class, you know."

"I don't believe in class barriers, Frank," she said. "Not between people when you like them." She lowered her eyes. "And I thought that you would be nice to go out with."

He thought that she would be just like he'd figured. A mousy spinster who'd wind up being an old maid. It was just like her type to tell you how much they loved working in the slums and how they liked people so much.

"I wouldn't stay down here for a minute if I didn't have to," he said. "There wasn't any welfare workers like you around when I was a kid. We were low-class brats then." He grinned at her. "Now I've come up in the world; I'm a low-class dish-washer."

Mary reached over the table and touched his hand. "Don't be like that," she said. "Don't be so bitter about the world."

"It's a lousy place to live most of the time."

"But there are so many beautiful things," she said, smiling. "Down here too. I see them every day."

Her fingers were soft when he turned his hand over and caught them in his palm. He held them almost hesitantly. "Okay," he taunted. "Besides you, tell me what beautiful things I could find in this neighborhood to brighten my day."

90

"Do you like children, Frank?" She did not pull her hand away.

"Wobble heads?" he asked. "Oh, I can take them or leave them. I never been around them too much. It wouldn't be too bad to have a couple of your own, I guess."

"They're beautiful," Mary said. "They're full of innocence and interested in everything. Even a garbage can is full of adventure for them. Have you ever seen the beauty in a child, Frank?"

He watched her. Have you seen them dirty-necked and grubby, with their pants full of crap and a headful of lice? he thought. And screeching their heads off when you want to sleep.

"I never paid too much attention to kids," he said.

"Or two young people in love," she went on, smiling still. "There were two at the last dance we had at the Path. I watched them standing near the door, watching the others dance and just their hands were touching, but you could see the love in their eyes when they looked at each other. They couldn't have been more than sixteen."

That was good old-fashioned hot pants you saw in their eyes, baby, Frankie thought. They were probably looking for someone to borrow a rubber from, so they could go down to your locker room.

He grinned at her. "I wouldn't know love if it bit me," he said.

"You will someday," she assured him. "But there are nice things everywhere, Frank. People are just afraid to look. They only see the bad things and stay in their shells."

"Like me, huh?"

"It doesn't take much effort to look, does it?"

91

"I've been looking," Frankie said. He held up her hand. "See what I found?"

"Ummm," she said. "You found a cloistered welfare worker who you did not believe would accept your invitation to go out." She squeezed his hand. "Why did you ask me? You looked so grim and irritated over the tray, and were so intent to shrug it off."

This dame's a nut, Frankie decided. I wanted to get in your pants, that's why I asked you out. I'm going to do that. You're ripe for someone to give you a big rush, and a line about this love-and-kids crap. I'm going to have you wondering where the cherry went in a month. A willing rape.

He looked at her long and carefully. "I don't know really," he lied. "I was lonely, I guess. I don't know many people around here and I didn't think I'd be lonely if I took you out. I'm not used to taking out a decent woman, Mary."

She ought to eat that up, he thought.

"The ones I usually wind up with aren't the kind I'd take to a movie."

After that there was a moment of silence. Then she said, "I don't know what to make of you. You're the first man I've been out with in months, and I find myself wanting to act like a schoolgirl around you. I don't trust myself when I feel like that."

He smiled his best smile at her.

"And I think that you should take me home now," she said. "I don't know if you'll ask, or even want to, but I would like to see you again. I'd like very much to see you again."

He had taken her home.

That's the kind of a lousy date that first one had been. If it hadn't been for his plan, he would have told her to take herself home. It had really been a big deal, holding hands. Not a feel even. Hell, he hadn't even kissed her when he got her to her pad.

That was the whole lousy date.

Frankie got up from the bunk and scratched his legs vigorously. He'd bet he *did* have the crabs.

He'd like to see that moron Hamilton find any mistakes he'd made during that first date.

Hamilton was considering his own mistakes just then.

He'd made the mistake of becoming a cop. There was very little that a cop could do on Saturday morning that would make the day pleasanter than Friday had been. True, it had been forecasted that Saturday would be two whole degrees cooler than Friday had been, but there was no consolation in that. You had to consider that being on duty twenty-four hours a day, seven days a week, made Saturday an unlooked-for event.

There wasn't much you could say for a day that people used to get away from work to do what they wanted. Doing what they wanted sometimes led to throats being slit and heads being busted. All of which made more work for Hamilton, who was already doing someone else's work.

Hamilton brooded about that. It wasn't bad enough that Kinsmiller had dumped a graveyard shift beef on him. He hadn't been satisfied with that. He had to top yesterday off by calling him into his office and chewing his ass over some punk's split lip. He hadn't hit that punk that damn hard.

You'd think he'd used a chain on Trumper or something, the way they'd acted. He really should have worked the punk over, and said he'd fallen down the steps.

93

That's one I owe you, Trumper, he thought. He wondered just who in hell Kinsmiller thought he was.

What is this? Just what in hell is this? A punk, a two-bit piece of garbage from the gutter who's been in trouble since the son-of-a-bitch was big enough to get his hand into a cash register. And he's got more rights than a cop has. He doesn't have to answer questions. I have to. I've got to explain myself. I've got to justify my actions to a lousy lieutenant.

Where the hell are *my* rights? *I'm* not booked into this station, but I got to answer goddamn questions when a punk don't. And who do they believe? Me? It's pretty damn hard to take when your own skipper tells you he's hearing a street punk's story better than yours. Coercing evidence, he calls it.

A slap in the mouth is coercion? He taught him some manners, that's all he did. Now he couldn't even question the punk without the lieutenant being there.

Kinsmiller would blame him if he lost this one. Don't question him alone, he said. Don't violate his rights. Don't threaten him. Don't come to me and say he's the one because he's got that punk smell. Sure, the lieutenant could smell it; he'd seen a thousand punks come through here. But don't say it to him, because the DA couldn't take that to a grand jury.

That was a lot of don'ts.

He could break that punk's story in half a day upstairs. But don't.

Just solve that murder, Hamilton sighed.

Considering all those don'ts, he was still expected to roll up his sleeves and tackle this investigation with hammer and fire, so to speak. Mister punk Trumper wasn't on trial; *he* was. He didn't have to get enough evidence to prove Trumper guilty; he had to get enough to keep his job.

94

It was a lousy situation. Trumper had two strikes against him—a prior sex beef and being on parole.

But I'm the one who's striking out. That punk will go free and I'll see nineteen years on the force shot in the ass for a brutality charge. Kinsmiller, Rawls—whose side were they on anyway?

He couldn't answer the question. He was sure of only one thing. Trumper was an oily punk that was guilty of something. It wasn't enough. He needed some hard facts.

A coroner's report is hard facts.

Hamilton had read the one on the dead girl as soon as it reached his desk that morning. There was only one piece of information in it that surprised him. Most of it simply irritated him.

There were a thousand suspects in this case besides that punk upstairs. That's what made the case so rank. It would be hard to prove that Trumper had done it, with all of those other possibilities.

The coroner's report didn't seem to help matters any. The girl had died between midnight and 2 A.M. Death had been caused by either of two blows on the head with a hammer-type object.

And what does that tell you? How do you cut the odds that are stacked in Trumper's favor with crap like that? He read the report for several minutes, then frowned and picked up the phone. There might be too many people involved with the case, but there was no excuse for the coroner to add to the confusion with such crap as a "hammer-type object." It could be important to know what that weapon had been when he searched Trumper's room.

And while he did not expect to find the weapon itself,

there was a chance that he could narrow things down by knowing exactly what the coroner meant by hammer-type object. What the hell was a hammer-type object? A golf club, a crowbar, how about a pistol grip? That's a hammer-type object, isn't it?

Aren't there enough problems around here without some white-coated idiot sending over reports that could mean anything? If they had said blunt instrument, he'd have accepted that. He would have known then that the coroner's office had no idea what had been used. But no. They had to prove how useful they were, and put down things like "hammer-type object." Which one of those idiots put that down in his report?

Clyde Baumgart had put it down in his report. Clyde was a dignified-looking little man who always seemed to have just stepped out of a funeral parlor. He was brisk and direct, with a rather lofty manner that in no way affected his deciphering of minute facts. He had the calculating sureness of a computer when he worked, and he worked with exactness. And with all this going for him, he did not like the telephone call he was getting from Hamilton.

"You certainly were very helpful this time, Clyde," Hamilton said. "I just had to call down and thank you for that report on Mary Blair."

"Oh?" Clyde said, detecting a note of sarcasm. "What is the problem, Hamilton?"

"Problem? Oh, yes, there *is* one little problem," Hamilton said. "I know that you are very busy people down there. And we certainly don't expect you to be the Dostoevsky of the lab reports. But would you please tell me what you mean by 'hammer-type object'? Could you explain that little problem?"

"The problem," Clyde said, "is that you are a prick." He

paused to let the revelation sink in. "In our opinion a hammer-type object was the murder weapon. That is what we think. That is what we put into the lab report. I believe you have enough intelligence to understand—"

"I understand that an idiot could have told me that," Hamilton cut in. "Will you please tell me how you reached that earth-shaking conclusion? Maybe I can use that."

There was a long silence at the other end of the wire. Then Clyde's voice came back cold and clipped. "To begin with, there are two bone penetrations in the left side of the victim's skull. These are approximately one and one-quarter inches apart. Each of these penetrations is approximately twenty millimeters across. The striking face of the object would be the approximate size of a hammerhead."

"Then why don't you say hammer in your report?"

"Because we don't know. We deal with facts, not assumptions, as you do, or theories if you like. The wounds could have been made by a hammer. They might also have been made by using the end of a piece of pipe."

"A pipe's not hammer-type."

"We have our reasons for saying that, if you'd like to hear them."

"Go ahead."

"Well, considering the force needed to penetrate the skull, a pipe or similar object would have continued on deeply into the brain. A hammer, or an object with a handle, would have been stopped by the handle itself, or by the widening of the striking object's head. These wounds were made by a hammer-type object."

"Any other possibilities?"

Clyde sighed. "Of course. Similar wounds could have

been made if someone wanted to mislead us. But I doubt if that's the case here."

"I'm always being misled," Hamilton said. "Go ahead. How?"

"I suppose they could have been made by holding a piece of pipe in your hand and striking with its end. The hand itself would stop the pipe from penetrating too deeply." He paused. "It would take a blow of considerable force. Does that clarify our opinion any?"

"Oh, sure," Hamilton said. "All I have to do is look for a hammer-type murder weapon."

"Would you care to be misled some more?" Clyde asked. "There are two points that we don't agree on down here. One tends to support a hammer as the murder weapon, and the other is purely theory."

"Go ahead, make my day complete."

Clyde was enjoying himself now, speaking in a patient but patronizing manner. "Point one is in the lab report. There was a chip of black plastic embedded in one of the wounds. We ran some tests on it and it's a high-strength plastic, the type used in tool handles and things of that sort. It is not a flat fragment; it could have possibly come from a plastic-handled tool, similar to a screwdriver or hammer handle."

"Great," Hamilton grunted. "And what's the other point?"

"The second point is open to argument," Clyde said. "And in fact it is the reason for 'hammer-type weapon' being in the report rather than 'hammer.' "

"I'm all ears."

"I'm sure you are," Clyde said. "But I don't think I have time to give you a course in orthopedics. So I'll ask you to view the girl's skull as an egg. What would happen if you struck

98

an egg with an object that had the striking face of, say, six millimeters?"

"A puncture in the shell, I'd guess."

"Correct," Clyde said. "You show great promise, Hamilton. But what would happen if you struck the egg again, a short distance from that first puncture?"

Hamilton studied the autopsy on his desk before he said, "Another puncture of the same size and shape."

"That is what we don't agree on down here," Clyde said. "The first puncture would have weakened the shell; it is a thousand-to-one chance that only another puncture would result at the second blow. But it is quite likely that the second blow would collapse the entire side of the skull, at least the area between the two blows. This isn't the case with the girl. There we have two clean punctures with very little collapsing of surrounding bone."

"The thousand-to-one chance?"

"If you like those figures."

"What do you like, Clyde?"

"Just remember that this is only my personal view," Clyde said. "I believe that both of the punctures in the girl's skull were made at the same time. That would account for the area between them being intact."

"What are you telling me?" Hamilton asked. "That I'm supposed to go looking for a two-headed hammer as a murder weapon?"

"A hammer-type weapon," Clyde corrected him. Then he added, "Of course, the same results would occur if you held two pieces of pipe a short distance apart in your hand and struck with that."

Hamilton sighed. "At the same time, huh?"

99

"That is my own opinion," Clyde said. "All right?"

"I'm sorry I called," Hamilton said. "I liked it better without two-headed hammers."

He hung up the phone and stared across the room blankly. "Now there's a red-hot aid to detection," he said aloud. "A goddamn two-headed hammer. It's a wonder that we catch anybody."

The desk sergeant looked at him in puzzlement.

Hamilton ignored him and read the rest of the report again before he turned his attention to the list of items that had been found in the girl's purse and were now in the property clerk's office.

There was a padlock key listed, but no key that might open the door to the social center. He would pick up that key before he went down to see Miss Kenton or Grewe. There had been lockers at the center, he remembered. He might find one that the key fit. He might also have Miss Kenton expand on her knowledge of Mary Blair's sex life. Considering the coroner's report, there was a great deal more to it than he'd learned yesterday. Also, in reading the additional information, it was beginning to look like that Trumper punk might beat the rap. He didn't like to think about that.

He put on his hat and went out through the gate in the partition near the sergeant's desk. "Tell the lieutenant I'll be back around one. I'll be at the Twelfth Street Social Center first," he said.

The sergeant looked up and smiled. "I heard he had you on the carpet over Trumper."

Hamilton stopped. "He didn't suspend me. Disappointed, huh?"

100

"Come on, Mose," the sergeant said. "I'm on your side, remember? You checking on that case?"

"Yeah," Hamilton said. "I am, like the book says, diligently seeking out the facts."

"Horse shit," the sergeant said, picking up a property envelope from his desk. "This is for your friend upstairs."

"What's in there? A pistol?"

"A hand exerciser, no less," the sergeant said. "One of those things you use to strengthen your grip. He sits around and squeezes it, and his hand gets strong."

"All he'll need a strong hand for is to play with himself when I send him back to the pen," Hamilton said. "The governor will be sending him letters of sympathy next."

"You think you can pin this on him?"

Hamilton's eyes were blank. "I'll pin it on him," he said. "One way or the other."

"I like a man with conviction," the desk sergeant said, grinning broadly.

"You like screwing donuts?" Hamilton asked, and headed for the door.

It was already hot outside.

8

The newspapers were killing Frankie Trumper.

Rawls didn't believe it. He read the morning paper again in his apartment. They were killing him, all right. They had him tried, convicted, and on his way to the death house. Printing things like "PAROLED RAPIST HELD IN SEX MURDER" wasn't exactly a promise of justice to come.

He'd seen some of the justice that Frankie could expect from the police. He had never really believed that people were like that. There weren't any Hamiltons on *his* city's police force.

But there were. He'd seen the results of third-degree manhandling with his own eyes. What would they have done if he hadn't shown up and asked to see Frankie?

It was goddamn unfair. The unfairness, as he saw it, was a twisted thing. A man had been caught, convicted, and given justice tempered with a chance of rehabilitation. And then he had been returned to society with a chance to adjust. The parole record showed that Frankie had adjusted. He had been ordered to live a normal life. How, then, could he be condemned for a crime he had already paid for?

And what do I do? Rawls thought. Do I stand by and let the law run its course? Stay on the fence until guilt or innocence is proved? Or do I go ahead and take Trumper's side

102

all the way, not just as his parole agent but as someone who is willing to help? Someone who will be there when he needs someone on his side? The man certainly needs someone like that with crap like these papers are putting out, and Detective Hamilton.

But what if he's guilty? How do you explain standing behind a guilty man? How do I explain not condemning him, for that matter? Where the hell does my responsibility end?

Who do you think you are? he asked himself suddenly. Who in hell are you to even think of not standing behind him? He is your responsibility. He was in society because you allowed him to remain there. So if—if he's guilty, then so are you, because you exercise the controlling regulations.

He did not like the line his thoughts were following.

He did not like the idea that he had failed in his job. The price of failure in the past had been more years out of men's lives. But if he had failed to do his job with Frankie, the price would be a bit higher. Frankie would go to the death house this time, and he would have failed to reach him, or recognize that he had not been blending into society as well as he had thought.

Two lives then—Frankie's, and the girl's.

But was it his failure? He considered the thought and grinned. He was, in fact, a little god. The law had delivered to him one hundred and twenty-seven lives to direct. He was therefore responsible for the direction those lives took. He was their guide.

Where had he guided Frankie?

How could you be fair about a thing like this? Or was the word square, as the parolees seemed to think? Being a middle-man was a damn poor place to play at being god. Well, he would not be a pawn for administering someone else's idea of justice. He would help Frankie because it was his job to have a little faith in men, but he would determine if that faith and help were warranted; he had to be sure of that in his own mind.

He folded the newspaper neatly with an air of finality. Then he picked up the phone and dialed the number of the public defender's office. He would see to it that Frankie Trumper did not get any more split lips that might help him change his mind.

At ten o'clock Saturday morning, Rawls was in the public defender's office at the courthouse. Howard Dolbee had continued to process the papers on his desk as Rawls spoke patiently about Frankie.

When he had finished, Dolbee glanced up and said, "When, and if, he's indicted and brought before the court, one of our attorneys will be assigned to represent him."

"He needs an attorney now," Rawls said. "He needs legal advice before he finds out he's talked himself into an indictment."

"I know," Dolbee said. "Almost all the convicting evidence in the cases we represent is gathered by the police prior to the charge and indictment being made. That evidence is sometimes of the type that would not be given if the defendant had been represented by counsel." He paused and looked up. "Confessions, incriminating statements, alibis that place the defendant at the scene of the crime rather than alibis for him. I know all about that. I'd like to see the public defender get as early a start on a case as the DA does. But the procedure is that I cannot assign an attorney to Mr. Trumper until he comes before the court and the judge assigns our office to defend him."

104

"By then he very likely won't need an attorney," Rawls said. "What the hell kind of a system is that?"

Dolbee waved his hand at the frightening pile of paper work on his desk. "You see this? I've got four attorneys to divide these between. Their calendars are full for the next three months." He shook his head and pulled his glasses off. "We have to ask the presiding judge for a three-month continuance at the preliminary hearing when we're assigned. That might give us time to prepare a case. We can't use our attorneys on a case that we might not even get."

"Is that justice?"

"We try. That's the best we can do. Justice is a nice word, Mr. Rawls. But from this end I'm willing to settle for a little mercy."

"Mercy?"

"A deal, Mr. Rawls. A cut in the sentence, in return for a plea of guilty."

"And what happens if the man is innocent?"

"We take the case to a jury trial if we can't get a deal. And we'll fight it the best we can. It might take six months between indictment and trial." He paused. "They usually can't make bond so they wait, or they plead guilty and hope for mercy."

"I'll be goddamned," Rawls said. "You mean that an innocent man would have to spend six months in jail just for a chance to prove he's innocent?"

"If he were indicted, pleaded not guilty at the preliminary hearing, and couldn't post the bond that the judge set, he would remain in custody until the case was heard. If we handled it, that would be between three and six months."

105

"And if he could afford to hire a private attorney to represent him?"

"He might get to trial within a month. He would have an attorney to represent him from the time of arrest, or as soon as he contacted an attorney."

"You're telling me—"

Dolbee held up his hand. "I'm telling you that we do the best we can. I'm telling you that while justice, in any form of the word, cannot be bought, it certainly can be hurried, by having money to hire an attorney." He shook his head doubtfully. "Justice may be blind, Mr. Rawls, but it is not deaf to the ring of a cash register. If I were charged with a crime, I would personally prefer to be guilty and have money rather than be innocent and trust in a noble concept."

"I see," Rawls said. "It's a pretty hard thing to believe, isn't it?"

"I've been at this job for a long time," Dolbee said soberly. "It is not so hard to believe. Truthfully, after reading this morning's papers, I think Mr. Trumper would be better off with you to deal for him."

"Me?"

"Don't act as if I spit in your face," Dolbee snapped. "They're going to crucify him—first the public, then the DA—and the DA's going to have to be asking for the death penalty by the time we get the case. By then we could maybe get him a life sentence for a guilty plea."

"I still don't—"

"The public is trying this case. They see a paroled rapist who murdered and raped an innocent girl who was working to help people like him. They are going to have a field day with him; he might just as well have murdered a police officer if he's

106

guilty. I don't see how he can get an unbiased trial in this city, let alone expect any mercy."

"He hasn't been indicted or even charged yet."

"That's why I say you have more chance of helping him now," Dolbee said. "How much time did he have on his old sentence?"

"He's served four," Rawls said. "That leaves the better part of fifteen years to do on that sentence. He's been paroled from that."

"Is there any chance that he's guilty?" Dolbee asked.

Rawls looked at him. "I suppose that there's that chance. There's a chance that you or I did it too."

"We're not charged with it," Dolbee said. "He might be, and I told you where that will likely lead. I suggest that you stop the ball before it starts rolling if you can. While the police are still not sure of getting an indictment."

"How?"

"Offer the DA's office a chance to save the taxpayers the expense of a trial. Offer to violate his parole now and send him back on that old charge. Fifteen years might seem enough to them while they're still unsure of getting an indictment. It won't be enough after they do get an indictment."

"No," Rawls said.

"You'll be pressured to do the same thing even if he's not indicted. Public opinion can be a strong thing, Rawls. People will want him off the streets because they have already convicted him. You'll be pressured to do it anyway; you'll be accused of coddling ex-cons and told to get tough, starting with Trumper." He picked up his glasses and put them on. "I'd see the DA if I were you."

"No. It's too unfair."

107

"But it's better than going to the death house or getting a life sentence, isn't it? Talk it over with Trumper anyway. If he's guilty, he'll jump at the chance."

"No," Rawls said again, and picked up his hat.

"I'm sorry I can't help you," Dolbee said. "I'd like to."

"Could you recommend a good attorney?" Rawls asked.

"I could. Why?"

"If he gets an indictment, Trumper will have had at least the same chance I would," Rawls said softly. "He'll get a defense, if it has to be against the whole damn city. Pressure and cash-register justice be damned."

Hamilton was not considering any kind of justice when he drove over to the welfare building. He was not considering the administering of laws as a point in the case either. The case had taken on qualities that could be accepted on only a personal level. He had committed himself to the theory that Frankie was guilty, and now there was a good chance that he was not. The lab report had practically eliminated Frankie in his own mind. Which might be good for Frankie and good for justice, but it sure as hell wouldn't be good for Hamilton.

Frankie had to be guilty, he thought. Or I might just as well turn in my badge. Kinsmiller will have me up on charges for sure. Brutal treatment of a man who has been proved innocent, he would say. He just couldn't afford to have Frankie proved anything but guilty.

Hell, he thought, he was guilty. Public opinion had him guilty. What was a little autopsy report against that? It didn't absolutely clear him; all it did was indicate a better suspect—or did he try to fit Frankie into some very unlikely shoes? Frankie

108

would have had to be the girl's lover to fit into that autopsy. How did you tie up a punk with a girl like that?

He had to do that or go after Mary Blair's lover. He couldn't do that and cut his own throat with Kinsmiller. Frankie had to be the one.

He had to hang a frame on Frankie, he thought. So what? The punk was sure to be guilty of something. It would be a public service to get him off the street—and Hamilton would keep his job.

He didn't need more evidence. He needed to know what evidence there was that pointed to another man. He would find that, and tuck it away where it wouldn't be found. It was just too bad he couldn't get rid of that one part in the autopsy. But maybe Frankie could be fitted into that.

A frame had to fit.

He remembered that the welfare center was closed on Saturday when he reached the building. He found an open bar on the next block that had a telephone directory.

Miss Dian Kenton lived in Fair Acre, on the west side of the downtown section of the city. Her apartment was in a cold-water flat that had been renovated—within the limitations of doing only what the housing laws demanded—and converted into an apartment house that had a dated look, despite the new cover of plaster and paint. Miss Kenton was waiting for him when he knocked, and asked him into a small apartment consisting of a bedroom, a living room, and a kitchenette, the compact type of kitchenette where you could move one step and reach all of the utilities. There was also a bathroom with a bathtub that had enameled plywood sides, to give it that modern square appearance and serve to hide the old-fashioned tub with legs underneath. Miss Kenton had furnished the apartment very simply. It was cool, and clean, and frilly, with a woman's fussiness. It gave Hamilton the feeling of being in a place where there are ashtrays but they are not to be dirtied.

Miss Kenton did not look much like a welfare worker this morning. Her hair was brushed loose, hanging thick and soft to her shoulders. She wore a white blouse and tan pants with a wide belt. She seated him on a low couch in the living room and said, "Can I get you a drink? Or is this an official visit?"

"I could use a drink," Hamilton said. "Official or not."

"I was thinking of mixing a vodka gimlet when you called. Is that all right?"

"Anything cold," Hamilton said. He watched her mix the drinks in the kitchenette. There was more of Miss Kenton to watch in slacks than there had been in the two-piece business outfit. She was full of surprises. She carried the drinks, cigarettes, and a table lighter back into the room, and set them on the glass-top table in front of the couch, then she seated herself next to him and sipped her own drink before saying:

"Two of my favorite vices, gimlets and cigarettes. I have quite a few vices for a social worker. What did you want to know about Mary that I didn't tell you yesterday? I understand that the police have made an arrest in the case."

"We have," he said. "But what we talked about yesterday keeps coming up. I'm going to talk to some of the kids that were at that dance today, and I wondered if you had remembered anything at all about the man she dated. You thought that she had a lover, but it seems odd that she never mentioned his name."

"Yes." Miss Kenton smiled. "But she was hardly in any

110

position where she would want it known which men she was sleeping with."

"Men? There were more than one?"

"There was one in particular, but I suppose that she went out with others. We never talked an awful lot about that."

"Did she ever talk about more than one man?"

"No, I just assumed that. We only discussed sex once really. The other things, what we talked about, came in just girl talk."

"Well," Hamilton said, watching her. "What did you talk about that one time?"

Miss Kenton hesitated. She pulled her legs up under her on the couch and leaned back, then shrugged. "Just girl problems. They're pretty much like boy problems that first time, aren't they?"

Hamilton tried to smile. He wasn't very good at it. People do stupid things. Honest, law-abiding, helpful people do things that they consider right, and are really a pain in the ass to the cops. It was perfectly all right to want to protect a friend's name, they thought. What they didn't understand was that a bright and shiny name is no great prize when you are dead. And holding back information might make him miss some facts that he wanted hidden properly. He didn't want any sexy facts turning up that might help Trumper.

Like the fact that the autopsy showed that Mary Blair had been ten weeks pregnant when she was murdered. Now there was a motivation for murder if he had ever seen one. It was going to be pretty tough to hang that on Frankie, let alone have some other sexy facts turn up that would point to someone else. It was a biological fact that Mary Blair had been spending some time with a man, and things being like they are,

111

he could assume that she'd had more than one roll in the sack with him. Which brought up questions like: Who was he? And was he frightened enough to let Frankie take a ride without making known his own intimacies with Mary Blair?

"I don't know what kind of problems a girl has that first time," Hamilton said. "I'd like you to tell me about that talk. It might be important."

This is a sexy interrogation, he thought. "If it embarrasses you . . ."

"Me?" Miss Kenton said, smiling. "I grew up in this city. I learned the facts of life from five neighborhood boys before I was out of grade school. I can't say that I even fought them very much. I think I was as curious as they were intent. It doesn't embarrass me, Mr. Hamilton, but it did Mary. She was still a virgin at twenty-five, you know. It bothered her very much. And then one day she decided not to be one anymore. The next day she was an emotional wreck. Sex that first time can seem awfully wrong when you think about it the next day. That's what we talked about; she couldn't decide why or what had made her do it. She was embarrassed that she had enjoyed it, which was more than most girls do the first time, and she wasn't sure it had been her own idea."

"Was she forced?"

"No. Not that. She seemed to think that it was a very strange experience. She came to me for advice about that."

"What did you tell her?"

"I simply told her that it was always a strange experience the first time. She must have accepted that, because she told me later that it was always strange for her."

"And she never mentioned the man's name?"

"Not once that I remember."

112

"Can you remember exactly when this talk took place?"

"Is that important?" Miss Kenton asked. "It's been months ago."

"It's important," he said. "She was two and a half months pregnant when she was murdered. I'd like to know when she started sleeping with this man. Did you know she was pregnant?"

"No. I didn't think that," she said. "I thought that she was having trouble with her lover, but not that sort of trouble." She bit at her lip for a moment, and then said, "I think it happened last April. But I can't be sure."

Hamilton watched her.

"Do you think that it had anything to do with her murder?" she asked.

Hamilton said nothing for a moment. "No, I don't think so. I think we have our man. I'm just wondering why that nameless lover hasn't made himself known."

I hope he doesn't make himself known, he thought.

"Perhaps he is afraid to admit that he has been sleeping with a murdered girl. People don't care to get involved with things like that."

"That would be my guess," Hamilton said. "I *am* sorry about this line of questioning."

"Oh, stop acting like I'm a nun," she said suddenly. "I've reached the age where life can be a dull, barren thing. I've reached it without any man setting off any fireworks with me. I think it might be too late for that. But I don't know."

"Well . . ."

"Did you expect something different from a welfare worker?" she asked. "Most people do." She smiled at him. "But we are women, not sexless machines in the welfare system, as

113

people stereotype us." She paused and sipped her drink, watching him over the rim of the glass. "I feel as any other woman does about men. I imagine Mary did too."

"I'm not stereotyping anyone," Hamilton said. "There isn't much that will surprise me after nineteen years on the force, but you learn not to type people because the clerk type can turn out to be an ax killer. The only type who stay the same are punks. Them you can depend on; they stay punks, right from juvenile detention to prison or the death house. I don't have time to type people like Mary Blair."

"And what do you think of me, Mr. Hamilton? Mose, isn't it? You told me yesterday at lunch."

He nodded. "I hadn't thought about it at all."

"I don't believe that. You don't ask people to lunch for questioning all the time, do you? I thought this visit today might be because you wanted to see me as well as ask questions. You're a funny man, Mose. You don't care much for people."

"Is that so bad?" Hamilton asked. "I'm a cop; it isn't my job to like people. My job is to enforce the law, and it's full of filth and indecency. I wade in people's dirt every day. I see people like they don't care to be seen, with all their rottenness hanging out. Should I like people, get all chummy with every punk or whore I pick up? I'm looking at the retirement end of twenty years of being a cop. I don't need to win the year's friendliest cop award to help me make it to retirement."

All I need is a frame for Frankie, he thought.

"And what will you have at retirement then—loneliness?"

"This is turning into one hell of a questioning, isn't it? That's the trouble with you damn women! You think having

114

friends and being liked is the whole world. I'll settle for doing my job."

"I know you're a hard-boiled detective, Mose, so why try to prove it to me?"

"I'm not trying to prove anything to you. I came over here to ask some questions. I don't understand people like you anyway. You work at the edge of the same crap I do. Doesn't any of it stick to your shoes? Don't you get damn sick and tired of it, like I do, and start to wise up that the fact is these people like living like they do?"

"That's not true, Mose. Anyway, we're dealing with children. They're not responsible for living where they do."

"A punk's a punk. Little ones grow up to be big ones. If they don't want to be one, they can grow up clean and get out."

"We have a terribly different outlook, don't we, Mose? We think so differently that it frightens me."

"Why should it?" He sighed and wagged his head. "Look, I'm sorry we got sidetracked like this. I've got a few more questions and I'll be on my way."

"You don't frighten me, Mose. I frighten myself. Ever since I met you at the center I've wondered if you're the one who could make those fireworks in me."

He started to speak and she held up her hand, stopping him.

"I was thinking of you when you called this morning," she went on quietly. "You can accept the terrible things, the sad things in life, and there isn't any room for anything else, nothing reaches you anymore. I thought I felt sorry for you yesterday, but it was more than that."

She looked at him searchingly. "Where were you ten

115

years ago, before it was too late for us? I think there would have been sparks then."

Hamilton watched her silently. He put his glass down on the table and folded his hands. Then he unfolded them and picked it up again.

Dian Kenton's eyes were suspiciously wet, a softness in her face. "You don't know how to handle this, do you? You're at home with crime, but not this, not something without lies or violence." She said it sadly.

"Well . . ." he began, and lost the words.

She moved across the couch and stopped, almost touching him. "I wish I'd never met you, Mose," she said. "Then I'd never have had to wonder about us."

She felt his hands touch her waist and their hesitant pressure. She touched the long white scar on his chin, following it with her fingers and pressing her hand against his cheek. "I'm not breakable," she said softly. "Try me."

Hamilton picked her up and carried her toward the bedroom. Frankie could wait for his frame.

9

By 1:30 P.M., the heat was back in the city.

It was obvious to anyone who had bothered to listen to the radio that the weather forecaster had been on the sauce again when he'd read his crystal ball and come up with the story that it would be two degrees cooler in the city on Saturday.

It was ninety-eight in the shade. That was three degrees hotter than yesterday, on September 16 yet. You couldn't tell anyone in the city that the weatherman wasn't on the sauce. The noon forecast had promised rain for Monday, not that anyone believed it, judging from past performances.

The city was wilting. It shimmered limply in distorted waves. The streets seemed to be glassy limp ribbons with oozing black threads of asphalt. The trees in the park on East Bagley Street were drooping in the windless air, and the lake lay like a hot sheet of glass with no offered coolness to the sweating citizens enjoying Saturday on its banks.

For the first time in his life Frankie Trumper found a point of agreement with the police. The East Bagley Street station *was* the hottest place in the city. And his cell was undoubtedly the hottest one in the cell block.

He had dozed during the morning, drifting into a restless series of naps, until he had heard the food cart being pushed up the corridor outside. He felt the heat in the cell pasting his

117

shirt against him in dark splotches of irritation as he waited for his tray.

There was a bowl of soup, a peanut butter sandwich, and a cup of coffee on the tray. He ate with a dull drowsiness clamped over his mind, and returned to his bunk. But the interruption had broken his spell of dozing and he lay on his bunk, moving only his eyes as he searched the blank ceiling and listened to the pigmy voice of a radio somewhere in the cell block.

They couldn't prove it, he thought. There wasn't a chance of them proving a thing. Nothing.

But why hadn't that lousy Rawls sent that attorney over yet? What if that stupid, pious bastard wasn't so stupid? What if he went and played along with the cops?

Sure, he was going to check his story, Frankie expected that, but there was nothing to find. Nothing to tie him in. Frankie sat up on the bunk and watched the portion of the cell block he could view through the bars of his cell. It was very solidly constructed and deeply quiet.

He felt a dribble of sweat creep down his jaw and, defying gravity by refusing to drip from his jawline, follow his neck until it was soaked up by his shirt.

You noticed all the small things when you were alone, he remembered. He had spent a lot of time in a cell. It was all part of their routine, he decided. They had questioned him and failed. Now they would leave him alone and let his mind work on him. They wanted him to wonder, and to worry, and to sweat.

He was sweating, all right. But it wasn't over this beef. He had it beat! Only there was something worrisome about sitting alone in a hot silence when you knew very well that outside the cage there were men searching, picking up threads, asking questions. Free and working to find a little something of a mistake that would solve the case satisfactorily and send him right to the chair.

Hamilton was that type. He liked his cases finished permanently. He was outside looking. Maybe Rawls was looking too; you couldn't trust those pious, square bastards. There hadn't been any attorney around, had there?

Frankie thought about the death house. He could play it hard with the cops, but who's kidding who? Nobody wants to take the black slide on a lightning bolt. They said there wasn't any pain in going to the chair.

How in hell do they know? Any of them try it? You could take that no-pain crap and shove it. It cooked your brain, didn't it? How the hell could that be painless?

He couldn't let himself think like that, he told himself. The next thing he knew he'd be copping a plea for a way out of the hot seat. That's how those bastards worked.

He rubbed his face and neck with his hand, and felt the sweat-freed grime on his chin roll into tiny rat turds of dirt. It's like a Turkish bath in here, he thought. A lousy stinking bull palace . . .

He stopped the thought, remembering that it was a lot cooler there than it would be strapped down in the chair, with a wet sponge under the bands on your arms and legs. And a big wet cushioned ring around your shaved head.

He couldn't shake the thought even though he knew they wanted him to sit and think about things like prison and the chair. Especially the chair.

Think about the chair, Frankie. Remember the stage shows the cons had out there every year? Every time there had

119

been a humor skit about the chair, hadn't there? Because the damn thing was there, inside the walls with them, and they wanted to show that it didn't bother them. They called it the Humble Machine, the Brain Buzzer, mostly they called it Big C, and everybody knew what was meant when they said a man was walking with Big C tonight.

Funny, huh?

What the hell had been the last chair skit he'd seen? He'd laughed like hell about that one. It had been real funny then.

He tried to remember something funny about the damn death house.

I'm not going to the chair, he remembered. I got this beat! I . . . got . . . it . . . beat!

They couldn't do it. Not when he'd been so careful. He could laugh at them—they'd never be able to put him into Big C. He was too con-wise for this sit-and-worry routine to work. He wasn't copping any plea.

He lay back on the bunk and listened to the hollow silence. And he remembered. He remembered the first night he'd been at the prison when a man had walked with Big C.

He had felt it in the air, a tenseness, a growing sense of something building around him. It hung close, a nagging irritation, rubbing his nerves until his gaze jerked about in furtive probings, seeking to identify that nameless something, and his back had itched like something was walking behind him, watching him.

And he refused to identify the tenseness he saw in the faces of the other cons. It had seemed to grow with the evening, pushing into the cell blocks until the talk gave way to a whisper, and at eleven-thirty the whispers faded to what sounded like the breathing of some waiting animal.

120

He had sat and watched the hands of the cell hall clock, and felt the presence of something else in the cell with him. At eleven fifty-five, the security guards had stopped walking their tiers, and the echoes of their steps faded, to leave a silence so deep that it made his ears ring.

He had watched the clock, holding his breath as the hands crept to midnight, and the lights dimmed across the prison. Thirty seconds passed in dimness before the lights brightened briefly, but only to dim again for a silently shrieking two minutes before they brightened again, and a sigh sounded like rushing water through the cell block.

He could not remember the name of the man who had gone to the chair that night.

It didn't matter, he thought. The cons will never hold a death wait on him out there. He wondered why the chair hadn't seemed important before.

He had never considered that. He had never thought that a little hump could lead to that. It wasn't like he'd planned to hurt her—just laying her was all he'd planned.

He supposed he could never explain that it wasn't rape either, if it came to that. Telling them how it happened would only cinch the chair for him.

Where was that lawyer! And Rawls, he's stupid enough to be out somewhere with the DA, telling him how bad he thinks the treatment is here. He'd be the kind to do that, instead of getting an attorney to keep the bastards off him.

Well, piss on him and his help. He only had two more days. Frankie couldn't wait to see the expression on Hamilton's face when he walked out of there Monday. Couldn't find anything, could you, bull?

Could he?

No. Mary had helped him there. She liked to do stupid things. Like going to places where there wasn't a chance of anybody she knew seeing them.

He'd almost dumped her on that second date, he remembered. Jesus, that mouse was a square. No feel, no nothing that first date. And she'd wanted to go to a movie and a Dutch-treat dinner on the second one. The goddamn bitch! He'd known she was just being bitchy by showing him that he couldn't afford to take her where she *really* wanted to go. He'd known she was just teasing him with that nice-girl act. He would have dumped her too, if he hadn't known for sure he was going to lay her. He'd been sure of that when he thought of the plan. He was going to show that goodie-goodie bitch how good she was.

But he had to play the game with her. Feed her a line until she trusted him enough to take him to her apartment.

He'd thought he had something going when she suggested the walk in the park after the movie.

Maybe she's the type who don't like taking guys to her pad, he'd thought. Maybe she wants a quick roll in the bushes.

The park had been filled with a spring newness that night. There was a balmy freshness in the air along the gravel paths, a freshness alien to a city that was beginning to harvest the smells of winter-hidden garbage now thawed and rotting in the alleys.

There was a newness in the white-green of flower sprouts starting to show in the dark beds along the paths, and in the budding branches of bone-white birch trees. Even the usually dark green spruce trees were newly dressed in a pale green and oozed a sticky sap that smelled of turpentine, adding a new tang to the air by the lake.

122

There was no doubt about it, the park was a pretty nice place after months of snow and slush. In the spring it was a place for lovers and old men who would never be lovers again, but could watch those that would, with a faraway look in weakened eyes. Even the muggers and the jack rollers stayed out of the park in the spring because of a lack of trade. As a rule, the park did things to those who visited it during the spring.

It made Frankie wonder what in hell people saw in parks anyway.

They were maybe okay, he decided as he glanced at Mary walking beside him. She had her hand looped casually through his arm and he could feel the firmness of her thigh brushing him.

He'd have to try her, he thought. Maybe he could get into her pants without doing what he'd planned. Maybe she was just a nature freak, and liked doing it in the park. He wouldn't be surprised if she was just a high-class tramp, playing coy.

She had on a tighter dress this time, he noticed. One that fit snug across the rump. As she walked, her hips moved tauntingly under the thin fabric. He liked to watch her walk, invitingly. You got your leg men and your boob men; he was a rump man himself.

It was nice and quiet down by the lake.

"What is this?" he asked. "A cross-country hike?"

"Just to those birches near the bank." She laughed. "It's my favorite spot."

"Man," he said, "I got a shoeful of gravel from that path."

When they reached the trees, he saw that the grass was already growing there, thick and carpetlike, not in hesitant patches as by the paths. They sat together and stared at the lights the city had spaced around the lake.

"Isn't it peaceful here?" she asked.

There's only one piece I'm interested in, Frankie thought. "Yeah, real nice," he said.

"It's still a little chilly out though," she said, moving over and leaning against him.

He had put his arm around her, turning her slightly to kiss her. Her mouth was cool, unmoving. He could feel her body tighten in protest, and he pulled roughly away. "What's wrong with you?" he demanded.

Her eyes were closed tightly. In the yellow glow of a near light he could see tears squeezing out from under her lids.

Don't blow it, Frankie thought. The lousy, teasing bitch. Wait until you can do what you planned. He started to move away but her arms went around his neck and pulled his mouth back. "Please, Frankie," she whispered against his lips. "Don't go so fast. Please give us time."

Then she kissed him, her lips warm and willing. It was a gentle kiss. Frankie liked it. He'd never been kissed like that before. It was easy to see that Mary was going to be one hot little lay when he got her going.

He could feel the hot craziness growing inside him when she pulled away and asked, "Better?"

His hand slid up under her breast. "Yeah," he said. "You kiss like you mean it."

"I do mean it," she said, and put her hand over his, pressing it firmly against her a moment before moving it back to her waist. "We have a lot of summer ahead," she said.

He moved away and fumbled for a cigarette. Baby, he thought, I'm going to make a three-way sex freak out of you

124

for this tease. I'll have you begging for it any way you can get it.

"Is that a promise?" he asked.

She squeezed his arm. "That's a threat, I think," she said lightly.

He could feel the gnawing pain growing in his loins. He glanced at his watch gratefully. "It's almost eleven," he said. "I'd better get you home."

She watched him. "Mad?"

He managed to grin. "I guess not," he said easily.

She sighed. "Good," she said. "Let's not rush anything, okay?"

It's closer than you think, Frankie thought. "I'll take you home," he said.

She put her arms around his neck again. "As soon as you kiss me," she said. "Then we'd *better* go."

He had taken her home.

That had been the second date. Some date, he decided, watching a fly buzz around the empty food tray in his cell. Some lousy date.

The bitch had got what she deserved. A lousy tease. First she goes and wants a Dutch-treat dinner to make him feel cheap. Then she acts like she's ready for a lay, and lets a guy work himself up. All he got from that date was a hard-on. He should have taken her then, and had it over with.

That's when he knew he could get her to take him to her apartment, he remembered. That's when he was really sure that he could work it on her. She wanted to, he knew. But she wasn't sure. He knew he could make her sure the next time.

He was watching the fly feeding in his tray when the guard

125

came to tell him that his attorney was there. That stupid Rawls was smarter than he'd thought.

When Hamilton left Dian Kenton's apartment that Saturday afternoon, he was considering that it would be stupid to put a loose frame on Frankie. A frame had to fit; it was harder to put a frame on a man than it was to dig up convicting evidence.

The trouble was, Frankie didn't fit into being Mary's lover. There was no way possible he could fit that punk into that. No court in the world would believe it possible that Mary Blair would get herself knocked up by a slimy punk like Trumper.

What then, damn it!!! It had to look like Frankie and not some unknown lover. He grinned to himself as he drove.

And here I am an unknown bed partner of one Dian Kenton. I'm beginning to think I'll wind up hanging a frame on myself if I get any more surprises like that. She may look like the girl-next-door type, but she sure is hell in the bedroom. He sighed contentedly. Maybe we can work something out when this mess is finished. If it is finished.

By Monday yet! He had to have the frame tight by then, or Frankie walked out, and he could kiss nineteen years on the force good-bye for some petty brutality charge. That's all Kinsmiller needed. He'd use that and those seven line-of-duty homicides to get him kicked off the force.

He wondered how Dian Kenton would feel about getting into bed with an ex-cop—a killer cop, they'd call him. His anger for Frankie ate at his mind again. He should have picked that bastard up himself. Then . . . His thoughts came in a disorderly jumble.

126

No!

Think about it, he told himself. He thought about it a great deal as he drove. He was used to death. He had ended seven cases with death, and investigated innumerable other deaths as a matter of course, an everyday occurrence. And he'd seen his fellow officers find a senseless death at the end of some punk's gun. He felt the idea growing in the back of his mind.

Cops died useless deaths, didn't they?

Punks killed their victims uselessly, didn't they?

So?

So isn't it about time some punk died for a purpose? Frankie was probably guilty anyway. That would finish the case . . . he'd make that retirement then. Nineteen years of punks.

Wait. He couldn't just do something like that. He felt a sudden chill creep up his spine.

What's happening to me? I've been a good cop. That slimy punk's got me thinking of murder! He felt the silent fury of the thought. A frame, yes, but not murder.

And then he remembered that sending a man to the chair with a frame wasn't exactly doing him a favor.

He considered that as he drove. The thought of not framing Frankie never entered his mind. There was only the question of which alternative would best serve the purpose.

It was a troubling question.

10

A parole agent was paid approximately six thousand dollars a year.

Any way you cut that figure up, it was not a lot of money for helping to solve the social-adjustment problems of more than a hundred men. It was not a lot of money even if that was all there was to being a parole agent. But there were some other, minor duties that came with the job.

Like being a one-man employment force. That was a minor task that came up pretty often, about twice a week in fact. Well, he could let them sit around the local pool hall all day. He didn't *have* to get them jobs.

And there was the small matter of playing matchmaker. You could get a reputation as a cupid hater in executing that minor duty. A parole agent didn't have to give any of his parolees permission to marry. But it took a little time out of his day explaining to a two-week parolee that he couldn't afford to marry a local hooker on thirty-two fifty a week, despite the fact that she was just the type of girl he'd dreamed of in stir.

But even that was easier than being peacemaker in a parolee's family problems. It seemed that every married parolee who came out into the waiting arms of his wife had suspicions that she had not been keeping her legs crossed as tightly as she had told him in her letters. The suspicions usually led to black eyes, and those led to the wife visiting the parole agent, and that led to . . .

Well, it was a wonder that parole agents had time to solve the social-adjustment problems with all those minor ones turning up. You had to be some kind of nut to want those minor duties.

Rawls wondered if he wasn't some kind of nut.

The attorney he had hired to represent Frankie had insinuated that before he'd taken Rawls' check. He had also informed Rawls that slow justice was nevertheless justice, and that the city's public defender system was one of the best in the country. These bits of information had not cost Rawls a cent. Nor had the revelation of the fact that he couldn't run a one-man crusade against the system.

What had cost Rawls money was his not believing a word of the advice. You could bury him under a pile of alleged facts proving that society was bettered by the system as it was, and you could put a head on the pile by proving that justice was served eventually through the appeal system. But from under the pile you were still going to hear Rawls protesting that justice wasn't served out well with a leaky spoon.

At least it wasn't going to be served to his parolees like that while he was their agent. He might just as well be their financial aide too, he thought. He was damn near everything else.

That's me, folks, Charlie Rawls. The easy-touch parole agent, labor manager, cupid chaser, and marriage counselor. It was just too bad he didn't get paid for all those jobs. He could have hired Frankie two attorneys then.

And he damn well would have done it! It disturbed him that the day's happenings so far had not gone as he had expected. The news media had not withheld any news because of Frankie's possible innocence. The public defender had not gone thundering to Frankie's defense. The public defender had advised a deal as an alternative. And a private attorney had suggested that it would be wise if he did not make waves in the pond since people were inclined to think that public servants should agree with public views. Not to mention the fact that the commissioner wasn't going to like the waves one bit. These were some pretty good reasons to develop memory failure and forget the whole matter.

Well, he didn't intend to make waves or rock the boat. He was going to get in hip deep in that pond and splash water until someone had to bail like hell to keep such a system afloat. He was going to splash water enough to float Frankie into his fair-share, by-the-book justice, which was the only type Rawls accepted as justice at all.

It wasn't that he had any great love for Frankie. And he certainly didn't want to buck an established system. But it was the principle of the damn thing. If Frankie got this kind of treatment, why couldn't Rawls himself get the same kind, why couldn't anybody get it?

Someone had to make waves or the pond would go stagnant. He wasn't just questioning justice for Frankie. He was questioning justice for everybody. He was questioning it for his faith in a hundred and twenty-seven men. They were his first cases and, goddamn it, he might lose every one of them on violations, but they'd know that he'd tried. And that might help the next ones he got, because they would know he was on their side when they were right. He would make waves for that.

130

He could make a hell of a lot of waves when he thought he was right. He was protesting a thing that he wanted to give to each of the parolees, dignity and fair treatment.

They'll make a hero out of you, he thought sardonically. They'll place the rear end of a horse on a slab in the park and dedicate it to you.

The humor in the thought did nothing to improve the taste that the morning's harvest of wisdom had left in his mouth.

There was one minor duty he had to perform in his role as parole agent. He would check to see if his faith in Frankie was warranted.

There wasn't any doubt about it, he decided. He *was* some kind of nut. You had to be to spend your Saturdays playing detective, when you spent the rest of the week doing everything else.

Frankie's rooming house would be a good place to start.

Rawls had never lived in a rooming house. Every time he went down to the district around Sunset Avenue he realized that he had not missed a thing by growing up in the suburbs.

He had not had the opportunity to get used to a building's smell, or to find out that a rooming house stank all year round, and when it was hot enough to melt the asphalt on the streets it really stank.

The stink of the building where Frankie lived struck his face like oily smoke when he went through the outer doors. It was the combined smell of urine, and rotting garbage, and dirty diapers. The smells of living, he knew. But when they were united with the dank smell of the building's age, and with the odors of past living, they made a stink that you didn't need

131

to smell: you could taste it when you breathed, and feel it against your skin. You really received full benefit of a rooming house's smell when you were unaccustomed to it.

Rawls paused at the rusted mailboxes in the outer lobby and read the nameplates. Frankie lived in 3-C. He pushed the button under 4-C, and read the name above the button.

Ethie Biglin had been a vague hope to Frankie when Rawls had asked him if any of his neighbors might have heard him in his room late Thursday night. The rooms on each side of Frankie were empty, but Miss Biglin lived directly across the hall. She might have heard him.

The buzzer released the lock and Rawls opened the door. It isn't that I doubt Frankie's story, he thought. But it would be nice to know for sure where he was Thursday night. It would really be nice to *know* that. Frankie had also told him that Miss Biglin was a carhop in a drive-in restaurant and performed other services in the back seat of cars when business was slow. Rawls had been amazed that someone had come up with drive-in pussy, as Frankie had so bluntly put it.

He stopped before the door to 4-C and knocked.

Ethie was wearing shorts and a halter when she answered the door. She was a tiny girl, about four foot eight, with huge brown eyes. She could easily have passed for a college student rather than a member of the city's newest corps of hookers.

Rawls remembered his own college days, and decided that she would be a delightful bundle to have in the back seat of any car.

"Miss Biglin?" he asked.

She tossed her head and smiled. "Yes?"

"I wonder if I might talk to you for a moment," Rawls said. "About your neighbor across the hall."

132

"You a cop?" Ethie asked. "I don't know anything about that creep anyway."

"I'm not a cop," he said. "The police force doesn't hire cops my size."

Ethie opened the door wider and looked at him, then smiled. "You are kind of small at that," she said, considering him. He didn't look like a cop. She had been a drive-in hooker for nearly two years, and was acquainted with most of the vice squad bulls. She had never had any trouble with them that she couldn't work off, and buying off big men in a back seat with a quick piece had made her resent big men in general. Rawls, now, was the type of man she liked to bed for pleasure. She liked her men small and active, and in a place where she didn't have to worry about a car driving up. Rawls looked like the active type. "What are you if you're not a cop?"

"I'm a parole agent."

"That creep's parole agent?" she asked, nodding at the door across the hall. "Public enemy number one over there?"

Rawls nodded.

She held open the door. "Come on in," she said.

The apartment was a casual mess, as though he'd caught her in the middle of housecleaning. It smelled strongly of disinfectant, and had a scrubbed look under the mess. She picked a pair of nylons off the back of a chair and nodded at it, before seating herself on the foldaway bed next to the wall.

"It must be fascinating work, being a parole agent, I mean," she said. "I never saw you visit that creep before though."

"I usually saw Frankie where he worked."

"That's what I gathered," she said. "I mean I would have remembered seeing *you* if I had."

133

"Did you know Frankie, Miss Biglin?"

"Oh, I knew him all right. I mean I couldn't help but know him, living right here like this. He used to stand right in his doorway and watch me leave for work. He'd just stand there, and squeeze that exercise thing he had and watch me. It made me feel creepy, having him just watch like that."

"He didn't actually do anything to you, did he?"

She smiled. "No," she said wryly. "He would just stand there and smile and watch me. I knew why he was watching me too. I used to give him a few extra wiggles when I went down the hall. I mean if he liked it that much to watch me every night, you'd think he would have had enough nerve to ask for some." She paused. "I'll bet you wouldn't just watch."

Rawls was looking at her legs. "Were you in your apartment Thursday night?"

"At what time?"

"After twelve, I guess," Rawls said. "The reason I asked was that I thought you might have noticed if Frankie was in his room."

"Gee," she said. "I don't remember. I mean I remember that I came home about one-thirty, but he doesn't stand in the hall and watch me then."

She put a cigarette between her lips and waited for Rawls to light it for her. "You know something?" she said. "He's a damn good-looking guy. Before all this stuff came out in the papers, I just thought he was a creep because all he did was look. He wouldn't have had any trouble with girls if he'd just asked." She shivered. "I wouldn't want him near me now, but the creep wouldn't have had any trouble with me before. I like men. I mean nobody thinks much about a guy just coming out and asking for what he wants anymore."

She looked at Rawls' face and crossed her legs. "He used to look at my legs, like you're doing."

"They're nice legs," Rawls said, looking at her face. They were very nice legs. He hadn't seen legs like that since he'd dated a dancer while he was still in college. "But I wondered if you happened to notice anything that might mean Frankie was home that night."

Ethie was silent for a moment. "That was two nights ago, right?"

"Yes."

"I mean two mornings ago, because I came in about one-thirty. I think you're right."

"What?"

Ethie kept smiling at him. "Now that I think about it. I remember that his light was on; you can see it under the door because the hallway is dark. And his radio was still on; I could hear that too. I wondered why he was up so late."

"But you didn't see Frankie?"

"No. He didn't come out to look then," she said. "If he was in there."

"He says he was in there," Rawls said. "I think he was telling the truth."

"Hey," Ethie said. "You mean that he might be coming back here? If he is, I'm moving."

Rawls grinned. "Because he admired your legs?"

She shrugged her shoulders. "Well, I don't mind that creep doing that so much," she said. "But I wouldn't want him coming over here some night. A girl likes to be asked, you know."

"I don't think he would."

"I'll bet that's what he was thinking about every night,

when he watched me," she said. "You should have seen the looks he gave me."

"Like mine," Rawls said, and leered pointedly at her legs.

"You're different. I'll bet you're not afraid to ask, as well as look. I'll bet you have all sorts of girl friends; just waiting to be asked, I mean."

"Millions of them," Rawls agreed.

She uncrossed her legs and leaned back on the bed. "Put me on that list too," she said. "Or are you the type of guy who likes big girls? I mean opposites attract, you know."

"I like small girls," Rawls said. "Small brown-eyed girls, in fact. But right now I'm concerned with Frankie."

She wrinkled her nose at him. "He might come back and ask before you," she said. "But I hope he doesn't—come back here, I mean. Anyway, all I know is what I told you. I hope it helps *you*."

"I hope so too," Rawls said, getting up. "Thank you for your time."

She stretched like a kitten. "You could really thank me if you wanted to," she said. "Do you know where the Car Dine Drive-In is, on West Second Street?"

"Uh-huh."

"Have you got a car?"

"It's right outside," he said.

"Good," she said, getting up and fingering the zipper on her shorts. "Turn your back while I change. You can drive me to work. I want to make sure you know where I work when you get ready to ask."

Hamilton was ready to ask a few questions of his own. They were unusual questions for a cop to ask. Questions like

136

how to make a number-one murder suspect disappear. He blamed it on existence. When you need a suspect, one usually doesn't turn up for months, but the first time you don't need one, there he is. A first-rate, number-one prime murder suspect. The motive fit, the time and place fit, all he needed was a little detecting to wrap it up.

It was all in the book.

Some cases just climb into your lap and solve themselves. Only it just happened that the solution wouldn't put Frankie back into the pen and get Hamilton a tear-up of that brutality charge. The solution would make it worse, if anything.

Hamilton was thankful that it had been he who had found the book. The caretaker of the apartment building where Mary Blair had lived was at first reluctant to open her apartment with his passkey. It took Hamilton five minutes to convince him, after returning to his car for the search warrant he'd obtained that morning. Hamilton believed in being prepared. He did not have any faith in people's willingness to help cops.

He had closed the apartment door in the caretaker's face and gone about his uncoplike search in the same manner he went about his usual investigations. He was looking for evidence that might weaken a frame on Frankie. Anything that might point to the man in Mary Blair's life. Love letters, men's shoes under the bed, aftershave in the medicine cabinet, a pair of men's pajamas in the closet; anything at all.

There had been no murder committed in the apartment, he knew. But there was a silence there, a silence that wouldn't be broken by a certain girl's private laugh, or her private tears; he knew this too. The silence in the apartment was edged with a hint of death. He stood in the center of the living room and glanced at the ironing board standing near the window over-

137

looking the street. There was a basket of clothing beside it, and a steam iron waited with its cord dangling near a wall plug.

There was an open magazine on a marble-top coffee table in front of the couch, and a pile of hairpins beside that. Through the bathroom door he could see the shower partition, with a slip and a pair of black panties hung over it to dry. The room created the impression that Mary Blair had just stepped out for a moment, that she would be returning to do the ironing, or perhaps curl up on the couch to read the unfinished story in the magazine. But death had a way of calling unexpectedly, and leaving unfinished things behind it. He shrugged and began to search the room, remembering Dian Kenton as he did; it was the same kind of apartment, fussy and neat, with knickknacks and starched frills. He noticed a fading smell of perfume in the room, a spicy, fresh smell that would be rigged with memories for a certain man in the city.

He found her letters in the bottom drawer of the dresser in the bedroom, and spent an hour sorting through them. There were no love letters or intimate notes, and no local return addresses on any of the envelopes. He finished with them and returned them to the dresser.

The box was on the top shelf in the closet. It was a green metal box with a padlock. Before he tried it, he knew that the key they had found in her purse would fit.

There were several savings bonds in the box, and a bankbook with an account figure of $750.32 in savings. There were also some older letters, which he studied closely, and a small address book that he put into his pocket. Then he picked up the other book from the box. If there was anything in the apartment to help Frankie, which he had no intention of doing, it would be in that book.

138

It had a white leather cover and gold-edged paper. There was a tiny gold lock on the book's front. It was one of those locks that are really not intended to lock anything, but are merely a small reminder that the book is a private thing, and not to be thumbed through casually.

Hamilton read the word engraved on the cover and tossed the book on the bed before he replaced the other items in the box and snapped the lock back on. Then he finished his search of the room and carried the book with him into the kitchen.

He found a steak knife in the drawer next to the sink, and stood staring at the single word on the cover a moment before he pushed the blade between the pages and cut through the leather strap below the lock.

There is nothing personal about a diary when you're dead, he thought. And if it had what he expected in it, he sure wasn't going to spread it around. Still he felt like a keyhole peeper.

So sue me, he thought, and began to read. He left the apartment five minutes later. The caretaker was surprised to have the detective stop at his apartment on his way out. The detective had seemed like the type who'd mess up an apartment and leave the door open when he left. First impressions are sometimes deceiving, he decided.

The detective thanked him politely and mentioned the fact that there was nothing in the apartment of interest to the police.

The caretaker believed him.

11

The cell block was beginning to stink.

The morning odor of an ammonia mopping had faded with the growing heat and was replaced by the smell of food from the kitchen downstairs and the street smell of gasoline and factory smoke. There was a growing smell of sweating men too. And because some of those men did not consider a daily bath a necessity on the street, their body odors ripened considerably in the muggy heat of the cell.

Frankie knew the smell. He lay on his bunk and added his own stink of fear to it. That's the trouble with carefully going over well-planned capers in your mind. After they have become facts, that is. Now, if you were worried about making mistakes, you'd have to think about every move you made before you made it, wouldn't you? Looking for mistakes later didn't help a thing. It only served to make you realize you had made some. No matter how carefully you planned, there was always that unknown element sneaking into your capers, small unexpected things, which could be fatal when you made plans as Frankie had.

He knew he had made a mistake. It was right there in the pocket of his trousers at his apartment. He remembered that little item after he talked to the attorney Rawls had sent. And now, since he couldn't just run over to his apartment and

140

correct the mistake, he lay in his bunk and tried to remember if he had made any others.

He was beginning to realize that there was the possibility that he didn't have this rap beat after all.

That would be his lousy luck, he supposed. With his luck he could marry a whore and she'd stop screwing. He'd had everything working for him. Rawls had been on his side, the attorney was drawing up a writ to spring him. And Hamilton couldn't find a thing to make an indictment stick.

But he could. All he had to do was go to the apartment and look in the pocket of the pants he'd worn that night. The indictment would stick then. It would stick him right in the chair at the death house.

He wondered if he should tell them about it. It might get him a life sentence instead of the chair by copping a plea. No. There was a chance that they wouldn't find it. The attorney would have him out on Monday if they didn't. He just had to hang on!

But had he made any other mistakes?

Was it possible that his simple plan had more holes in it than a sieve? He'd been very careful with Mary, really playing the role. But what about Iggy? Was he a mistake too? He'd been curious about the stuff, hadn't he? He'd been wondering just who in hell Frankie was dating that was worth that much trouble to get in her pants.

Iggy Domovic was a junk dealer on the avenue, which was a polite way of saying that he was a fence. It was his business to know who was buying and who had something to sell. And when the hot goods made their journey from buyer to seller through Iggy's hot little hands, he picked up a ten percent cut from both sides. Iggy would deal in anything that had a market value. He paid close attention to market trends like a depression-minded Wall Street speculator. If Iggy couldn't get it for you, it couldn't be had in the city.

Frankie remembered his talk with Iggy in the bar where he did his business. He'd made Iggy a lot of promises to get that stuff. Mary had invited him to dinner at her apartment, he remembered, and he'd gone to see Iggy. That supper was going to be the time when little miss fancy-pants got laid. It would be about time too; he'd dated her for two weeks already without so much as a feel. And Iggy was the man to see to help him correct that.

"What do you want that junk for?" Iggy had asked. "Tail is easy to get."

"Not this one," Frankie said. "Man, this bitch is cold."

"Yeah." Iggy grinned. "That's the trouble with you rape-os; always wanting some piece that don't want to play. If you got that much of a case for her, why don't you just take a piece? What the hell, you think I got nothing to do but run around town looking for junk like that? A lousy twenty-buck package won't even pay my gas money. I got to run over to the Mex section to get that."

"Can you get some or not?" Frankie wanted to know.

"Yeah. I can get some. I can get some junk that will make a rock want to screw. Them spicks use it when they got a reluctant doll they want to break into a cat house." He paused and chewed at the end of his cigar. "That Spanish fly can really make a nympho out of some of them. Especially the ones who want to do it anyway."

"So get me some, Iggy."

"For twenty bucks!" Iggy said, acting as if he wanted to spit on the floor. "You got me mixed up with the Red Cross or something. You think I do business for kicks?"

142

Frankie watched Iggy drink his beer. "Man, you do business for a fin. I know guys you pushed and pimped for and never made more than a buck off the deal."

"Yeah," Iggy said thoughtfully. "Yeah, but that was steady business. This is a one-shot deal."

"Maybe not," Frankie said. "Listen, this chick works in an office. That's one of the reasons I want to get her sleeping with me. She's got the keys to the building sometimes."

Iggy considered this for a long moment. "Office building, huh? Lots of typewriters and office equipment, huh?"

"Thirty or forty typewriters at least." Frankie grinned. "I figure on laying her for a while, until I get a copy of the keys made. Then I can just walk in there some night and clean the place out."

Iggy hesitated. "What place is this?"

"My business," Frankie said. "Don't get nosy, Iggy, or you'll be getting a broken jaw fixed."

"Don't get excited, kid," Iggy said. "If you get the keys, I could set it up for you. All you'd have to do was deliver the key. I could probably move some typewriters." He glanced around the bar. "I could give you ten bucks on each one we move out of there—no risk to you. You supply the key, that's all."

Frankie grinned. "How about my Spanish fly?"

"Well," Iggy said, making a big show of being generous. "This is a little different then. You got to bed this broad to get the key, then I'll see you get the stuff for twenty. Just remember me when you get the key."

"Good stuff?" Frankie wanted to know.

It was Iggy's turn to grin. "Like I said, you get some of this into her and she'll wear you out. She'll think she's got the hottest pants in the city."

143

"Get it," Frankie had said. "I'll be there to cool her off."

Frankie couldn't see where he had made any mistakes with Iggy. He hadn't told him her name or where she worked. He felt a small sense of relief. He hadn't made any mistakes there.

There was only that lousy key.

That could get him the chair. All those lousy cops had to do was search his pants at the apartment and there it was; a big red tag on the son-of-a-bitch too. It was better than a signed confession; it could connect him to the building and Mary.

He sat up on his bunk and stared through the bars at the window across the cell block. It was hot and bright out there. Hamilton would be out there looking.

Monday, Frankie thought. The lawyer said a writ would get me out Monday if they couldn't tie me in. A big hot-shot lawyer with that if-they-couldn't-tie-me-in crap.

Frankie puckered his lips and spit deliberately at the wall. He supposed that lousy Rawls would want him to kiss his ass for a year because he'd sent him. It sure would make a fool out of Rawls if they found out, or found that key. . . . It would make a dead man out of Frankie.

He watched the hot sunlight outside and thought about the chair. He kept staring out through the window, aware that his hands were trembling, but unable to stop them or the fear growing in his mind.

Rawls felt guilty about playing detective. He felt as though he had offered his hand and said "I'm your friend," and was now adding a silent "maybe" to it.

But what could he do? What in hell could he do?

He drove east on University in the late Saturday traffic.

144

He had found himself driving toward the Fourteenth Street Hash House, where Frankie worked, without intending to. Was he adding a silent "maybe" by checking Frankie's story? Was this his way of showing his faith now that he was committed to his proclaimed beliefs?

He'd practically shouted it from the rooftops, hadn't he? Innocent until proved guilty. That's the law, a basic right. I believe in it, he thought.

So why in hell am I playing detective then? Who am I to judge, if Frankie gets that basic right? There shouldn't be any question; it's my job to see that he gets it. Why do I have to prove to myself that he deserves what he already had by law? It's not mine to give.

I'm a goddamn crusader who wants to doubt his cause because it turns out to be an unpopular one. He grinned bitterly to himself as he drove. Boy, is it unpopular.

He could always say that he just wanted to help Frankie with his checking. He was responsible for him, wasn't he? But that wasn't the reason. The reason was simply that he had to know more about Frankie before his own faith in the man was beaten down by public opinion.

Is my own faith in men that weak? he asked himself. Is it so weak that I need proof to back it up? And where does it start to fall apart under pressure? Where do I say I know it's not right, but better him than me?

Stopping for a light near the hash house, he lit a cigarette. Well, he decided, he might be the one damn crusader in the city with a weak faith. But that was better than having no faith at all. He was on Frankie's side, doubtful or not.

He parked his car in a darkening parking lot half a block beyond the hash house and walked back wondering if Frankie's unpopularity had lost him his job. It wasn't hard to admit that it wasn't much of a job. It was, in fact, a very poor job, but it served the purpose of keeping Frankie employed.

The hash house itself was a purpose-serving establishment. It was the one place around where a man could get a hot meal for fifty cents. And when fifty cents was all a customer had to spend on a meal, he wasn't apt to complain about the quality of the hash. The place also served as a neighborhood hangout for the switchblade set. It kept them off the streets, or you could say it gave them a place to plan their current activities, such as moll-buzzing, purse-snatching, block rumbles, and such boredom-breaking things as bum-burning and cop-baiting. Activities such as these were generally only planned at the hash house. It wasn't very often that entertainment walked in unexpectedly.

The hash house possessed all the qualities of any other café or diner in that section of the city. Its windows had the same unwashed look, there were just as many cracks and chips in the countertop. The eight stools in front of the counter showed their share of padding through wear holes and knife cuts. The same knifework was in evidence on the four booths against the wall to the right of the door. In all, it was a pretty average hash house, with the usual blaring jukebox and, tonight, the usual Saturday crowd of kids. There were eight boys in the booths when Rawls opened the door. That's a crowd for a hash house.

The owner of the place was a Greek named Papas. He was a fat man with piggish eyes. Rawls wondered if the man had changed his dirty apron since the last time he'd been in to check on Frankie.

Rawls headed for a stool at the near end of the counter and sat down as Papas came over and said, "Well, if it ain't Mr. Rawls. You didn't come down here to see your boy, did

146

you? 'Cause if you did, you'd better find a place with bars on the windows; that's where he's at."

Rawls smiled. "No," he said. "I've already seen Frankie, Mr. Papas. I'd like to talk to you about—"

"Nothing to talk about," Papas cut in, holding up his hand. "I've had nothing but trouble since I hired him. He's finished working in my place. Who needs a real rape-o around?"

The boys sitting in the nearest booth were watching them now, Rawls noticed. "Mr. Papas," he said patiently, "I explained to you that Frankie would be subject to an occasional police pickup for questioning when you agreed to hire him. You said that it didn't matter."

"That was before."

"He's been doing his work, hasn't he?"

"Yeah. But how much work is there in washing dishes and delivering coffee once in a while? I don't need a rape-o to do that. I don't want any more like him around. It's bad for business; people been coming in asking how come I hire a rape-o when their kids need the work."

Two of the boys got up from the booth and walked over to the counter. Rawls watched Papas move off to serve them. He guessed the boys' ages at around sixteen, the age when T-shirts, tight Levi's and shaggy hair were the uniform of the day down here.

"So no more okay," Papas said, returning. "You talked me into it once. Give him a break, you say. Now look what it got me when I do. Don't expect me to hire any more. Makes me feel like it's my fault that he got to that Blair kid."

"That hasn't been proved, Mr. Papas," Rawls said. "Frankie hasn't been charged with anything yet. Not a thing."

"That ain't what the cops say," Papas offered. "There was

147

a dick in here today who figured Frankie was a sure bet for the chair after he talked to those kids over there."

"Why was that?"

Papas shrugged. "You figure it out. I tell him that this girl came in here once in a while, and Frankie delivers coffee where she works." He smiled thinly. "I'll bet that rape-o didn't tell you that he knew her."

"That's right," Rawls said. "But he told me that he knew who she was."

"No kidding?" Papas said. "I figured he'd lie like hell about that." He shrugged. "It don't make any difference to me. I still don't want him working here, even if he did get out of this. You tell him that when you see him."

"If that's the way you feel."

"That's the way I feel."

Rawls glanced at the group in the back. "What did the boys tell the police? About Frankie, that is."

Papas shrugged again. "Who knows? Why don't you ask them?" He pointed to the booth, and called, "Hey, Patsy. Man here wants to see you."

A heavyset boy with a build like a boxer leaned back in the booth casually and studied Rawls for a long moment. "His legs ain't broke, are they?" he asked. "He wants to see me, he can come over here."

The rest of the group grinned as Rawls slid off the stool and walked back. Patsy was obviously the leader of the group. He was a flat-faced boy with big hands and a hard face. There was an air of arrogance in the way he slouched back into the booth and asked, "Who're you, boss?"

"I'm Mr. Rawls."

"Yeah, but *who* are you?"

"I'm a parole agent."

148

"How about that," Patsy said. "Boys," he said to the others, "we are in the presence of Big Brother today. Be real polite to Big Brother, 'cause he might have you on paper someday."

"Let's hope not," Rawls said, grinning.

Patsy looked up at him and then nodded to the boy seated across from him. "That's Sleepy," he said. "Know what he was just telling me?"

Rawls waited.

"He was just telling me that a guy had to be two things to be a parole agent. You had to be too lazy to work and too scared to steal." Patsy smiled. "That true, Big Brother?"

"I'll let Sleepy figure that out for you," Rawls said. "Why do they call you Patsy anyway?"

" 'Cause I ain't," Patsy told him. The others grinned in agreement. "What's your beef with me, Big Brother?"

"You talked to a police officer today, right?"

"Yeah, I talked to a bull this afternoon."

"About Frankie Trumper?"

"Yeah, I talked to a bull about a rape-o by that name, I think. What's it to you?"

Rawls paused, then he said, "Okay, Patsy. You've impressed your friends now, so why don't you cut the wisecracks?"

Patsy looked around innocently. "Boys, was I making any wisecracks? Do I have to impress anyone?" He smiled at Rawls. "All I did was answer your questions, Big Brother. A guy can't be telling everyone what he tells the bulls about a rape-o, can he? I wouldn't want it to get around that I'm a stoolie or something."

"Look, Patsy," Rawls said. "I'm trying to help Frankie. I want to see that he gets a fair deal."

149

"Well, well," Patsy said. "A goddamn rape-o rescuer. You mean you ain't looking for a reason to send him back to the pen?"

"Should I be?"

"That's your job, ain't it? Sending them back."

"My job's keeping them out," Rawls answered. "So how about it?"

"He wants to save a rape-o," Sleepy said.

One of the boys in the next booth looked over the top of the seat and grinned. "Save one for me. I'd like to have my own private rape-o."

Slowly Rawls searched the grinning faces around him. "I don't think you kids understand," he said. "I'm trying to get a man a fair deal from the police and courts. And you think this is a goddamn joke." He turned to walk off.

"Did Miss Blair think it was a big joke, Big Brother?" Patsy asked, and waited until Rawls turned back. "Nobody is joking, boss. If you help them send him to the chair you'd be doing him a favor. I'm personally going to make him wish he was dead if he gets out of this." He kicked Sleepy's leg under the booth. "Take the guys and blow, Sleepy. You go tend to business while I talk to Big Brother here."

Rawls said nothing as the group broke up, then he slid into the booth.

"You want to know what I told the bulls, huh?"

Rawls nodded.

"It was anything else, I wouldn't give them the right time of day. I don't stool on anybody. Ask the guys that. But this is different. We liked Miss Blair. You ask them over at the social center. We'd go over there for a dance, and we never had no trouble when she was on." He paused and searched for words. "She treated us like people."

150

"I'm sure she was a fine person, Patsy," Rawls said. "But what about Frankie?"

"She was a lady," Patsy went on, "and she wasn't always bossing us around when she was at a dance. That's why I told the bulls what I did."

"What was that?"

"I seen that rape-o talking to Miss Blair outside the Path once."

"At the what?"

"The Path—you know, the social center. I mean I seen them with my own eyes, setting there, and him looking like he was ready to jump her."

"But what do you think that proves?"

"Proves? It proves like the bulls said. He knew her, didn't he? It proves he was trying to get a little, maybe, and she being a lady wasn't going for it. So I told the bulls this creep probably killed her 'cause she wouldn't give him any."

"So you think Frankie's guilty because you saw them talking together once."

"I know I saw them," Patsy said. "The bulls believed me."

"They would," Rawls said, and grinned wearily. "It doesn't prove anything."

"I'll tell you something else," Patsy said. "You should believe me too. We have a little bit of trouble with the bulls around here, but you never see any of the guys hurting a lady like Miss Blair. And just in case they don't send him to the chair, there's a lot of guys around here that ain't going to like anybody who helps that rape-o. Nobody likes a rape-o. You know what I mean?"

"Not really," Rawls said. "Spell it out for me."

"Well"—Patsy shrugged—"you know. Guys get busted

151

off parole every day, don't they? You wouldn't want no rape-o running around after your sister, would you?"

Rawls studied Patsy's face for a long time before he stood up. "I don't think Frankie has anything to worry about," he said carefully. "But thanks for the talk."

"You're going to help him?" Patsy asked.

"That's my job."

"That's what we figured you'd say," Patsy said. He sat there and grinned as Rawls walked out past Papas, who, for some reason, was shaking his head as if he was trying to tell Rawls something.

It seemed as if there were a lot of people in the city who were trying to tell Rawls something. The problem was that he wasn't listening right. He was going by the book. It is all very well to go by the book in an ideal situation, but ideal situations only turn up in books. Ideally he would be charged with the care and supervision of twenty men. Count them. Twenty. In that situation he could be absolutely sure of his reasons for supporting one of his men. He was a college-trained social worker, wasn't he? With twenty men he could possibly reach a fair understanding that would allow him to make reasonable decisions about them.

That was the trouble with the book way of doing things. It dealt in ideal situations. It did not tell you what to do when you had six times that ideal number of men to supervise. It did not tell you there are times when situations turn clear black-and-white rules into varying shades of gray that called for varying degrees of decisions. Rawls did not exactly know what in hell he was doing trying to apply book solutions to reality situations. He only knew that he was right according to the book. He felt that the city was dealing Frankie a black hand, and automatically wanted a spotless white solution to replace it.

Unfortunately, it was an unpopular cause. And while unpopular causes might occasion only verbal retribution from polite society, they received a bit more attention down in the Sunset Avenue area.

Unpopular causes were a slap in the teeth down there, and they were not met with verbal reprimand. They were met with a slightly harder slap in the teeth, which could possibly cure any crusader of his liking for unpopular causes. It is positively amazing how quickly a man can abandon a cause after some brass-knuckle therapy. There is nothing like a kick in the groin to make a man see the light.

Rawls had no idea what Papas was trying to tell him, when he left the hash house and walked back toward his car in the early-evening dark. He was concentrating on Frankie's problems and assuring himself that everything he'd learned had no bearing on innocence or guilt.

He did not become aware of the boys until he reached his car. It was dark enough in the lot to blur the figures leaning on the car next to his.

They waited until Rawls had spoken a soft greeting and reached for the door handle of his car before they hit him across the back with a tire iron.

It was a little late for him to wise up when the red darkness exploded inside his skull.

The boys spent fifteen minutes giving Rawls the message that parole-agent beating was a better pastime than bum-burning, especially when an unpopular cause was involved.

Frankie's cause was definitely unpopular.

153

12

When Hamilton left work Saturday afternoon, he had accomplished all he could toward his particular idea of solving the Blair case. He had questioned everyone connected with the case. He had confirmed the alibis given. He had searched both Mary Blair's and Frankie's apartments. His typed report indicated that he had found nothing during his search.

He had eliminated all other suspects but Frankie Trumper in his report, and in effect placed Frankie into a circumstantial frame that he hoped would be hammered tight by public opinion. He had neglected to mention Mary Blair's pregnancy in his report. That was in the autopsy, and if the DA wanted to read the autopsy he would ask for it. There was no use in calling attention to the pieces that didn't fit, and that mysterious lover didn't fit into Frankie's frame. Hamilton couldn't very well dispose of that evidence, but he could ignore it.

It was the first case he'd ever had where there was too much evidence. He was accustomed to digging out facts for airing, not covering them up. He had kept Mary Blair's diary in his car because it would be nice to know what facts he was covering up.

After he had glanced through the diary at her apartment, Mary's lover was still a mystery. She had not written his name into her intimate recordings.

That figures, he thought. After all, it was her diary. She knew who he was. She hadn't needed his name written on every page. You could hardly expect her to foresee a homicide detective sitting in an easy chair with an after-dinner drink of bourbon and reading her diary as though it were research material for a new exposé novel.

A diary is a very personal thing. There were writings in the diary that did not make sense to Hamilton, but were perhaps freighted with memories for Mary Blair.

There were several entries that Hamilton read with interest and considered as Frankie's hammer for breaking the hoped-for frame. The first was dated April 12.

Cold today, but so lovely to see the snow gone. I'm excited this evening—a date. He's an impossible man for me, good-looking in a rough-diamond way. I wanted to touch him. I wonder if he will be the one? I think there must be something wrong with me to be a virgin yet. Must rush. I will wear the pink dress for him tonight.

Enter one lover, Hamilton thought. Now if she had written down that she'd met an oily-haired punk with all the class of a dead pig, I'd have this on Kinsmiller's desk in two minutes. He wondered how in hell she'd managed to stay a cherry that long. This kid was too good to be real. He continued reading:

April 13
Typical day at the center. Mrs. Jackson's case is a nag. I've seen the same there several times. I'm sure she's living with him. Four children already and her husband gone—nobody seems to care where. If only I knew how to ask her. Or should I suggest that she might visit the clinic Tuesday? A birth-control class then. Her choice, but should I advise it? Must ask Dian about that. Last night was lovely. He seems so lost that I wanted to hold him like a child. A child! That's what's wrong with me—what do I need with a

155

child? I don't know how to act with him. He's the strangest mixture of emotions, angry with the world, I think. Yet he held my hand as though he could be gentle. I hope he will be. I told him that I would see him again—a surprise for me. Perhaps I'll see him during a delivery today.

Now there's a bit I could use on Frankie, Hamilton thought. He delivered coffee there. Too bad he doesn't fit the rest of this crap. He's a strange mixture, all right—a sex freak and a punk. I'd never be able to tell Kinsmiller that Frankie held hands gently. The only time that punk held a girl's hand was when he was trying to drag her into the bushes.

He laid the diary on the arm of his chair and finished his drink. There couldn't be more than a dozen delivery men that went to the center on that date, he supposed. He could check.

No. If he did, Kinsmiller would want to know why the check was made. It had to be Frankie; he couldn't be looking for someone else.

He mixed himself another drink before he sat down and picked up the diary again. The next entry of interest was dated April 16.

Spring is here. Everything is starting to grow again. My Easter lily by the window is late again this year; no green thumb. I think it will do better if I find it a larger pot to plant it in. What's wrong with me? I bought a very, very low-cut blouse to wear for him, but I chickened out, and wore one of my old ones instead. I want to be near him. But I'm frightened about the way I felt when he kissed me. I will wear that blouse for him next time. I'm a hussy at heart. I thought of buying black panties when I bought the blouse. For him? Who else? Blame it on the spring urge to mate, blame it on something. I'm twenty-five and frightened of it. How do you choose a lover? I don't understand him. I've just realized that I don't care. I am beginning to think that I will buy those black

156

panties. A new world outside, and inside me too. I think I will invite him to dinner here soon.

It was obvious to Hamilton that Mary Blair had purchased the black panties. He sighed and put the diary down again. What the hell am I reading it for? he wondered. All I'll get is eye strain. Besides, if she does name him in here, I'm not going to do anything about it. She got laid, and in the process she got pregnant. It was as simple as that. There wasn't any use in reading a personal account of it.

Goddamn it! He didn't want to know who her lover had been! He had his killer. He didn't need a lover suspect to drag in for Kinsmiller to use in busting him off the force.

He picked up the diary and carried it across the room to his desk. He hesitated a moment before he unlocked the drawer, fingering the gold-edged pages. Then he shrugged and placed the diary inside.

That's it, he thought as he locked the drawer. That's it! Cut and dried, it has to be Trumper on this beef. Him or me. A punk against nineteen years of my life. The punk has to go.

Who in hell wants to spend Saturday night reading a diary anyway? He picked up the phone on his desk and dialed Dian Kenton's number. He smiled as he waited for her to answer. It would be a better way to spend the evening.

Rawls could easily think of better ways to spend the evening. He awoke in darkness, seeming to drift up from a dark place, and as his mind drew near the gray edge of consciousness he became aware of the pain. He found the gray haze at the brink of wakefulness an uncomfortable place. He hurt like hell, and he could not at first remember why. And

157

when he did, he could not understand the sudden viciousness of it. Being right did not help him understand why he was lying face down on hot asphalt with his own blood stinking, sticky glue under his face, and raw waves of pain creeping into his mind. He fought the pain and raised his head, blinking his eyes open to clear the numbness and shock from his mind. He pushed himself up on his elbows and stared at the street light in the front of the parking lot before dropping his face into his hands to explore the crusted, sticky pain. His groping fingers found the exposed flesh in the gash above his eye and his tongue explored cheeks shredded by kicked-in teeth. Encountering the sharp edges of three broken teeth, his tongue recoiled from the exposed nerves.

The pain in his back was a dull ache of bruised flesh as he got to his knees and rested against the car. He suddenly realized that he was absolutely alone in the lot, and that nobody would help him if there were any second thoughts about the beating, along the lines of doing a better job.

It wasn't every day that someone had a chance to work over a parole agent. But why? It had to be more than helping Frankie. Or did it? Things like this weren't in the book. He could hear the sounds of traffic on the street. He had to get home. Concentrate on that.

Frankie wasn't responsible for this. It wasn't his fault. He kept telling himself that as he struggled painfully into his car. He listened to the words echo through the red haze of pain in his mind as he drove. If there had been any doubt in his mind before about justice for Frankie, it was gone. He would be less than a man if he backed out of this now.

Some people are just poor listeners. Some people are just the contrary type that knuckle therapy doesn't work on. It hadn't worked on Rawls, though he would certainly be the first to wish that any messages for Frankie would be given to him personally from now on.

He would be listening to what people were trying to tell him now. He would be hearing them loud and clear. But nothing would make him agree with what was being said. It was in the book in black and white, wasn't it? It was also emphasized with some red now.

It took him an hour to reach his apartment, where he viewed the red emphasis written on his face. And in the back of his mind there was a nagging little doubt beginning to grow. A small worrying thought of whether it was worth it.

13

Traditionally the seventh day of the week is a day of rest. Ask anybody.

On the seventh day he rested, right?

It was the week's seventh day, and no matter how tradition would have it, it was not a day of rest around the East Bagley Street station house. Around there nobody rested. It was like that three hundred and sixty-five days a year. You could always depend on work if you happened to be on the duty roster for Sunday, rest day or not.

Lieutenant Kinsmiller happened to be on duty. He had long ago reached the conclusion that in order to avoid a pile of paper work on his desk Monday mornings, he would have to spend some time at the office on the traditional rest day. He had developed the habit of driving his family to church near the station house and doing his paper work before he picked them up after services.

He considered the schedule a workable one though it sometimes clashed with the view his wife had on church attendance. He had explained it to her at least a million times. It seemed that every clerk and typist at the courthouse downtown spent their weekdays on coffee breaks or doing some leg-watching at the water cooler. And when Saturday descended on them, they started an attack on the week's paper work in an effort to clear their desks. And every request, memo, order, or report from that week would reach the station house at once.

It was also Kinsmiller's opinion that his detectives were developing the same habits. His men worked all week, however, and while they worked they made mysterious marks in their notebooks that it would take a five-man team of code breakers to decipher. Kinsmiller believed that the owners of those notebooks were sometimes confused about what they had written. They therefore spent a good part of Saturday deciphering their notes and heaping painfully typed reports on his desk.

So who wants to come to work on Monday morning and face a pile of work like that? Kinsmiller didn't.

Ask his wife.

He had driven her to church at ten o'clock, and reached the station house shortly thereafter to dig into the pile of work filling the in-basket on his desk. It took him twenty minutes to reach Hamilton's report on the Blair case. He studied it with interest and disappointment. It was the sort of report that, in itself, could maybe receive an indictment vote when the DA carried it before the grand jury.

He did not doubt that in this case an indictment would be issued, but not wholly on the report. Public opinion demanded an indictment, and it was reasonable to assume that Frankie Trumper would be indicted on one count of first-degree murder and one count forceable rape.

It was also reasonable to assume that Kinsmiller should delay filing departmental charges against Hamilton until the case was tried. He couldn't very well file charges against a man who would be in the public eye. The public would be wanting to know if Hamilton was an effective detective, and if he wasn't they would want to know why.

Jailhouse politics were a bitch, Kinsmiller acknowledged.

161

But it was a known fact that he could not bust a successful detective off the force. People were willing to overlook a thing like slapping a suspect in the mouth if the final results were the conviction of a murderer.

Kinsmiller would have to wait. He sighed and wished Hamilton would voluntarily get to hell out of his station. The best he had been able to do was order that another detective be present during any questionings Hamilton undertook at the station.

He found the priority-stamped envelope from the DA's office in his basket and wondered about it as he broke the seal. DAs do not usually have time to send correspondence to precinct houses. In all likelihood the DA couldn't remember offhand the names of his precinct officers. The priority envelope was addressed to Kinsmiller and lettered: "PRIVILEGED INFORMATION."

Kinsmiller read the enclosed carbons and swore as only a precinct skipper can swear, seventh day or not. Then he read them again, and swore some more before he picked up the phone and told Hamilton to come into his office, and he didn't care if he was busy. He wanted him in his office.

He waited in tight-lipped silence until Hamilton entered the office and slouched into the chair before the desk.

He stared at Hamilton and sighed, saying, "I read your report on the Blair case."

Hamilton nodded.

"Do you think the DA will get an indictment on it?"

"It's all in the report," Hamilton said. "Trumper will fall apart like wet toilet paper on the stand."

"He might, knowing the girl and all. Probably his attorney would have had him plead to a lesser charge after all the

162

publicity this would get." He paused. "That about what you think?"

"I think he's guilty." Hamilton grinned.

Kinsmiller rose from his chair, pacing between the desk and the window. The room was silent as he stopped to stare at the city from the small window. "It could have happened like that," he said at last. "He could be guilty. I want you to re-member that." He turned to face Hamilton. "It doesn't matter one damn bit what any of us think he is now." He walked back to his desk and picked up the carbons. "You know why?"

Hamilton shifted uneasily in his chair. "Go ahead."

"Because you couldn't conduct an interrogation properly after nineteen years on the force, and because you couldn't keep your goddamn hands in your pockets." His voice was hard and flat. "They're not trying for an indictment."

"What?"

"That's right," Kinsmiller said. "You gave him an out, Hamilton. You put him back on the street, free, with your lousy temper."

"How the hell—"

Kinsmiller held the carbons out across the desk. "And that's not all you did. Do you know what this is?"

Hamilton took the papers and glanced at them. "It's a writ."

"That," Kinsmiller said, stabbing his finger at the carbons, "that habeas corpus was taken before Judge Morton yester-day. Read it—it will give you an idea of how you screwed this up." He paused and stared at Hamilton. "Read that son-of-a-bitch!" he ordered. "Maybe you'll learn something about the laws you're supposed to be protecting!"

Hamilton stared at the writ and read:

163

SLADE COUNTY
MUNICIPAL COURT

In the original matter:

Frankie B. Trumper, Petitioner
v.
State *et al.,* Slade County, Joseph Kinsmiller, Respondent.

Petition for Writ of Habeas Corpus

TO THE HONORABLE JOHN W. MORTON, JUDGE OF THE ABOVE NAMED COURT

Wesley R. Ringstad, Attorney for the petitioner herein, respectfully represents and says:

1.

That he has been retained to represent one Frankie B. Trumper who is now presently confined and restrained of his liberty in the East Bagley Street Police Precinct Jail and Station House by one Lieutenant Joseph Kinsmiller, Superintendent thereof.

2.

That said confinement and restraint is illegal and unconstitutional;

(1) In that petitioner's arrest was without probable cause, warrant, or other valid execution, judgment, order, or degree.

(2) In that statutory law provides only for a seventy-two-hour investigation detention without filing a formal charge against him, and that said statute is in itself contrary to the principles of the Fourth Amendment to the United States Constitution and is therefore null and void.

(3) In that during the course of the aforesaid illegal and unconstitutional confinement the petitioner is being subjected to cruel and unusual punishment within the meaning of the Eighth Amendment to the United States Constitution, where he has been physically beaten and abused by one Mose Hamilton, Detective First Grade, Homicide Division, Metropolitan Police Department.

(4) In that his rights under the Fifth and Sixth Amendments

164

to the United States Constitution have been violated where he has been denied access to counsel prior to interrogation, and where he has during said illegal detention been subjected to continuous interrogation and threatened with further criminal process arising out of the investigation of hearsay accusations.

(5) In that his rights under the Fourth Amendment to the Constitution were further violated where subsequent to his arrest his person was searched and where his room was searched without probable cause therefor.

As to all said enumerated causes and reasons, and such grounds as the Court may consider which are not specifically stated, the petitioner seeks the following relief:

(1) That an order issue immediately granting the petitioner a prompt hearing to inquire into the cause and pretense of his confinement, or in the alternative and from the record herein he be restored to his liberty without further delay.

(2) Further relief is requested for the issuance of an order of restraint prohibiting said Mose Hamilton from unwarranted harassment as has been demonstrated from these acts. That all ostensible police authority exercise their power within the limits prescribed by statute and by the state constitution and by the United States Constitution. That as an added security to the petitioner and to the public welfare and safety, this Court order the suspension from active duty of said Mose Hamilton, and that the Grand Jury be impaneled to investigate the brutal, illegal, and unconstitutional conduct of law enforcement as exemplified by these acts and by the prior record of this officer.

Dated: September 16, 1967   Respectfully Submitted:

Raymond Dorral

Attorney for Petitioner

Hamilton stared at the writ blankly, feeling a chilling clamp of fear grab at his guts. They had to indict Trumper. Hadn't he made it obvious that there were no other suspects? Didn't those idiots know that they couldn't spring a punk

165

because he'd got a slap in the mouth? What was this? They couldn't spring Trumper and act as if Hamilton was the one going on trial. Could they be that goddamn stupid, after all his work? He'd framed Trumper good, damn it! They couldn't spring him on some petty crap.

Steadying his hand, Hamilton tossed the writ back on the desk and lit a cigarette. "How'd you get that, Lieutenant? The DA sending carbons of a punk's bitch sheets around now? They can toss that out and still indict—"

Kinsmiller shook his head. "It came from Judge Morton to the DA, and the DA sent it over here with this." He held up a second set of carbons. "Do you know Judge Morton?"

"Should I?"

"You will after today," Kinsmiller said. "He's one of the toughest judges on the bench when it comes to constitutional rights and police tactics. He's the one who put five city police in the pen for shaking down some whorehouses last year. It doesn't matter, but it's likely that Trumper's attorney arranged to bring the writ before him; he heard the case in his chambers yesterday afternoon."

Kinsmiller paused and watched Hamilton with mixed emotions, then handed over the other carbons. "He issued this order. Before you read it I'm going to tell you personally that you're finished at this station. I'd toss you off the force right now if I could do it. I'll let the commissioner do that when he gets my report. As far as I'm concerned I'm a witness to every charge in that writ, and I'll personally question your past record. It's going to look like hell for me to do that, but I'm going to add a violation of my orders and a recommendation of tossing you out for good to the commissioner."

166

"Just a minute! Who the—"

"I'm running this goddamn station!" Kinsmiller said. He was leaning over the desk now, and there was a white, pinched look to his face, as though he was just holding himself in control. "I'd personally take you upstairs and lock you up if I could. You're a party to this crime, the way I see it, because you're setting Trumper free with your stupidity. We might have convicted him. I'll see you off the force if I have to resign, because of the dirt I'll dig up on you." He paused. "You've hurt this station and every cop in this city, Hamilton. Now read that order and get to hell out of this station until Monday when it becomes official."

Kinsmiller glared at him a moment longer before he walked out of the office.

Hamilton watched him go, staring at the door after it had closed behind him. The bastard, he thought. The lousy bastard. He glanced at the carbons of the court order and read:

SLADE COUNTY
MUNICIPAL COURT

Misc. No. 494

September Term, 1967

Frankie B. Trumper, Petitioner
v.
Slade County et al.,
  Mose Hamilton,

BEFORE JOHN W. MORTON, JUDGE OF SLADE COUNTY MUNICIPAL COURT

This matter comes before the Court upon application for a Writ of Habeas Corpus, and is a first application therefor.

167

The files reveal that petitioner has been arrested and is now confined without charge in the East Bagley Street Precinct Jail.

It is alleged that the petitioner has been unconstitutionally denied access to his retained counsel. It is also alleged that petitioner has been unconstitutionally denied his rights under the Fourth Amendment to the United States Constitution where he was arrested without probable cause and without valid warrant issued by a magistrate upon proper proceedings required by statute and the United States and State Constitutions. Alleging further violation of Constitutional rights where he was and is being subjected to police tactics which are abusive to physical and mental welfare of the petitioner. That a search and seizure process has been executed contrary to Constitutional guarantees, and further violations are alleged within the meaning and scope of the Eighth Amendment to the United States Constitution, and a disregard for State Statutory provision as they relate to an arrest for investigative purposes which in itself is alleged to be an unconstitutional practice.

It is clear from the record before the Court that no hearing is necessary to determine these issues separately, or collectively, since a bare examination reveals that a flagrant abuse of police power and circumvention of the Constitutional securities is manifest.

It is therefore the order of this Court that the Clerk of Court cause and prepare an order granting the relief requested in the petition for Writ of Habeas Corpus, and that petitioner be restored to his liberty without further delay and no later than 10:00 A.M. the 18th day of September, 1967.
It is so ordered.

As a second cause it is further the Order of this Court that Detective First Grade Mose Hamilton be suspended from active duty and be relieved of all authority. That such suspension shall remain in effect until the conclusion of the Grand Jury investigation of these matters is reached.

The Slade County Attorney will forthwith formulate and pre-

168

pare the necessary files and records and convene said Grand Jury, not inconsistent with this Order.

Filed this 16th day of September, 1967,

By the Court

Louis A. Coolidge, Clerk of Court

John W. Morton
Chief Judge
Slade County Municipal Court

And that, it seemed, was that.

Hamilton dropped the papers on the desk and walked to the window. He looked out past the gray buildings, that were at last freed of the brassy glare of the sun, toward the city's horizon, where the black threat of a storm was building. He stood gazing out in the distance for several long minutes before he left the office and the station house, drove down toward Sunset Avenue and spent the seventh day getting drunk and wondering: What is this? What the hell is this?

"What the hell do you call this?" Cochan was shouting into Rawls' ear over the phone. "You hire an attorney! You give incriminating statements against a police officer! You personally get yourself involved in this and the DA is hot as hell about it."

Rawls rolled over in bed painfully and wished that Cochan would stop shouting into his ear because his head hurt like hell already. It looked like hell too, as he'd seen when he got out of bed once during the morning to shower and had looked in the mirror.

"He's my case, Herb. I'm personally involved with all of my cases. I can't do my job without being involved. The DA can get hot at the police if he wants someone to get hot at. All I did was protest for one of my men's rights."

"You can't do your job properly when you're involved," Cochan said. "You have to be objective about them."

"I'm being objective."

"The DA doesn't think so. He's already called the commissioner. He's calling it personal involvement and he's proving that Trumper was ordered free by technical faults. He's proving that the facts of the case haven't changed a bit— Trumper would have been indicted but for police procedure and your involvement."

"He's proving all that?"

"He's telling the commissioner that. I'm sorry, Chuck, but you really put your foot in it this time by hiring that attorney. The DA is wild as hell about that. The judge suspended the investigating officer, you know. Now the DA wants to know what we're going to do about Trumper, since we have obviously decided to take over police duties."

"What did the commissioner say?"

"He said enough to make my ears ring. Technicalities aren't a good reason for a possible killer to be free."

"Possible innocence is," Rawls said.

"Then leave it to an attorney to argue or prove that!"

The line was silent for a moment.

"Chuck? You still there?" Cochan asked.

"I'm here."

"Well, what—"

"Wait a minute," Rawls cut in. "I'm getting pretty damn tired of people telling me what I should do with my cases. And I'm damn tired of hearing that a man's rights are technicalities, and that everything I've been telling my cases is a bunch of crap. I've got too damn many, but I'll run them by the book, or I'll damn well know the reason why."

"We'll talk about it Monday."

"Don't hang up," Rawls said. "There's one more thing."

"I'm here."

"Don't pull Trumper's file on me."

"Chuck—damn it!"

"Don't turn him over to someone else to violate. I mean it. You transfer that case on me, and I'll raise hell all the way to the governor."

"I'd be doing you a favor if I did."

"Don't do me any favors," Rawls said. "I've got an investment in this case."

"Yeah," Cochan sighed. "The attorney's fee."

"More than that," Rawls said. "Call it an investment of faith, blood, and money."

"Blood?"

"Yeah, my own. I'll tell you about it tomorrow, okay?"

"Okay," Cochan said. "You sure ruined my day for me." He hung up and Rawls twisted around carefully and dropped the phone back on its cradle.

And now he might be responsible for the technical freeing of a murderer, huh? Well, for all of that, he might be responsible for more than a hundred known criminals being free. So what the hell was he worried about?

Only of being wrong, he told himself. Jesus Christ, what if I'm wrong after all of this? He knew what the fear was that he had to control. A risky thing to hang his future on, that faith. He could be wrong, but what was he supposed to do?

It wasn't in the book.

171

14

Frankie considered Sunday in jail as a bitch. There wasn't much to be said about any day in jail, but Sunday was the worst.

They only feed you twice, for one thing. They gave you slop at nine and slop at three, and let it go at that. You'd think they would at least feed you three times a day. That little diversion helped pass some time. The third meal meant that he didn't have to sit and think for a few minutes. He'd been doing a lot of thinking.

He sat on his bunk and listened to the cell block. The place was as quiet as a mouse walking on cotton, he decided. He picked up his hand exerciser from the bunk and began to squeeze it systematically. The worst part of Sunday was that there was too much time to think. He could see it was cloudy outside by looking through the cell block window. Even that didn't help. It was still hot and breathlessly quiet in the cell. There was no one around to talk with about the weather.

Think about something good, he told himself. Don't think about that lousy key in your apartment. Think about something real good.

Mary Blair had been real good that first time, he remembered. There was nothing like that had been, making her want to do it and still trying not to. It showed what kind of a tramp she really was.

Frankie remembered how good it had been when he'd finally got her to take him up to her apartment for a drink.

It was one of the nicest apartments he'd ever seen. Nice and neat, not like that hole he lived in. Even the apartment smelled like her. He enjoyed the smell while she mixed the drinks.

He wondered how much junk he'd have to give her to make her start wanting to take her pants off. That lousy Iggy had got him the Spanish fly, all right, but how much of the crap did he use? Jesus, he didn't want to give her too much. She might get wise to that. Maybe even die from it or something.

Relax, he told himself. Even if she did wise up, she wasn't going to yell rape. That's how most of the bitches were. They really wanted it anyway. Usually all it took was getting it in before they started fighting to keep it there.

So how much?

Just thinking how Iggy said she'd act made him start feeling like he had when he'd grabbed that first girl. It better work, he knew, because he felt that way. He was getting some tonight, and he wasn't getting twenty years for it either! He'd give her enough to make her rape him.

He put it in her first drink when she was sorting records to stack on the phonograph. Then he watched her and thought about how miss fancy-pants was going to be wanting something more than a necking session in a few minutes.

She came back to the couch and picked up her drink. "I'm sorry I can't offer you anything but gin, Frank," she said. "I don't drink very much. I wouldn't have this here, but a friend drinks it, and I thought I'd try it once."

173

"It's okay," he said, holding out his glass. "I'll drink anything. Cheers." She touched glasses with him, and barely tasted her drink.

Drink it, you bitch, he thought. He leaned back on the couch and stretched, held out his arms, and said, "Come here."

She moved over against him, holding her glass carefully, and rested her head against his shoulder. "Mmmm," she said. "Like the movies, huh? I'll bet that looks funny—us necking like in the movies."

"Who cares?" he said.

She giggled. "We're too old for that." She sipped her drink and looked at him solemnly. "Thank you, Frank."

Frankie looked at her.

"For being so patient with me," she explained. "You have been very patient, and understanding."

I didn't want you running to the law, he thought. Not knowing tonight was coming, you lousy tease. "Drink your booze," he said, "because I'm going to kiss you and I don't want you to spill it."

She finished her drink and grimaced as he grinned at her. He hoped she wouldn't notice how his hands were sweating.

"Um. Terrible stuff," she said.

It better work, Frankie thought. That stuff had better work. He could feel the heat creeping through his body as he pulled her abruptly against him, kissing her mouth almost viciously. Her eyes held an expression of amazement and a whimper came through her clinched teeth. He twisted his body and pinned her against the couch, his body a driving hardness against her. He could feel her whole body go vibrantly tense. She twisted desperately.

"No. No. Please."

174

He kissed her neck and ear, his mouth hot and eager against her, while her hands pushed vainly at his arms. He fought down the urge to beat her into passive submissiveness. He couldn't risk that. Why didn't that junk work? he wondered.

He held her tightly with one arm and dropped his other hand to her blouse, fumbling at the buttons until his hand was inside against her breast.

"Frank . . . please don't. Oh, please, please, please."

She sounded like a broken record, he thought, feeling the wetness of tears on his neck. He kneaded the breast with impatient fingers for a long while, finally feeling the bare nipple grow hard against the fondling. He could feel the limpness creep into her, as if she knew that her body was betraying her.

He moved her down on the couch before his hand dropped to her skirt.

"Please . . . please . . . please," she kept repeating, but her arms were around his neck and she was pressing against him crying as her legs opened to his hand.

Then he relaxed the pressure on her and moved slightly away. Her eyes were slightly glazed and she came to him without hesitation, her hands helping him build the hunger in her.

He'd been surprised how that junk worked, he remembered. She'd still put on that crying act, even while she helped him get those black pants off.

She had, in fact, damn near killed him. And he remembered that he had reminded himself not to give her so much the next time. Or the time after that.

It wasn't rape, he told himself. It was better than rape because she was a real sex freak when he'd given her some. And the next morning she acted like she couldn't believe it.

He'd enjoyed that too, telling her what a hot little lay she was. She never pulled that crying act in bed after that first night; she saved it for the times when he'd call her a nympho.

That stupid bitch probably thought she was; she probably thought a Spanish fly was in Mexican slacks. She was so stupid that she never did figure it out.

Stupid.

Stupid enough to pull that love crap on me.

Stupid.

He hadn't really intended to hurt her though. He liked her.

If only she hadn't been so stupid.

Frankie decided that thinking about Mary wasn't such a good way to spend Sunday after all. It made him think about other things—like the chair.

Hamilton walked from his car toward his apartment with the precise step of a man who knows he has had too much to drink and would like to hide the fact.

He would have to hide the fact that he was going to kill Frankie Trumper too.

He supposed he had known all along that he would have to kill him to make the freak's frame stick. It was pretty hard to frame a live man with a wise-ass lawyer and a punk parole agent backing him. It was an entirely different matter to frame a dead man.

A dead man with convicting evidence on him anyway. A dead man wasn't going to start yelling to some lawyer about a slap in the mouth. A dead man was just going to lie there with evidence in his pockets and let the facts speak for themselves. And let Hamilton speak for himself.

176

And because he was going to be the only witness to the resisting-arrest shooting, there wasn't going to be anyone around to question his word. A police officer's word, backed up with evidence, against a dead punk and his past record.

Let's see you constitutional-rights your way out of that, Trumper, he thought. Let's see you file a goddamn writ on that. That's what you punks call holding court in the street, isn't it? And a .38 slug is one unbiased son-of-a-bitch. No reprieves, no writ, no suspended sentences from a slug. Just one dead body and a closed case.

He'd still win this one, he thought. This was his whole life riding on a case. Nineteen years of punks like Trumper. Nineteen years of crawling around in the slime with it, of catching them and watching them get away with it, and catching them again to have some idiot judge say shame on you, son, and slap a light sentence on them. And they kept coming back.

Trumper wasn't coming back from this one. And he wasn't going to take a twenty-year retirement away over a split lip either. Trumper wasn't going to do anything but die.

He wondered why he hadn't figured it like that before. Well, he knew why, he guessed. He wasn't the kind of cop who just went around shooting people for nothing. You had to have a reason for shooting even a punk.

He figured he had a pretty good reason.

After all, he was protecting society, wasn't he? And Trumper was a threat to society any way you looked at him. So maybe he didn't do this one. How long would it be before he did one like it? And if Hamilton let himself get suspended off the force, who in hell was going to be protecting society then? Guys like Kinsmiller and Rawls? Trumper would get

177

away with raping half the city with guys like that protecting people.

It was all very clear when you thought about it like that. He was doing everybody a favor by killing Trumper. He'd probably be saving some girl from getting raped, besides saving his retirement.

He'd killed seven punks for less reason than that, he remembered. They wouldn't like his count rising to eight. But they couldn't bust him off the force for it. Maybe they'd let him retire early when he showed them that Trumper was guilty. Just a little planted evidence and a dead punk would do that. They could frown all they wanted, screw them.

He was doing them all a favor.

He climbed the stairs to his apartment and thought about it.

They were springing Trumper around ten in the morning, he remembered. He'd have to do it right after that. He'd have to act like he had a hunch that Frankie'd be trying to get rid of anything connecting him to the girl, and he'd watched him because of that.

Hamilton sighed and let himself into his apartment. Suspect resisted arrest and attempted to escape, he'd write in his report. And was shot by arresting officer during the attempt. That would be it. They'd find the evidence on Frankie. Period. End of case.

Simple. They might even apologize to him for the suspension. He hung his hat and jacket on the hook near the door and walked into the small kitchen, where he began mixing a drink. He knew that he didn't need a drink. But he was going to mix a strong one, and sit down and drink it. Then he was going to mix another strong one, and drink that too.

He did not want to think too much about it. He knew that he was going to kill a man tomorrow, there was no doubt about that. There was no choice—him or the punk. It had to be the punk.

But you had to admit that it was pretty hard to just up and decide to kill a man after being a cop. Maybe not the storybook, pat-'em-on-the-back type cop, but a cop just the same. He had, on occasion, been a brave cop. He had faced death for no more reason than a small pay check and a lot of dedication to what he thought was his duty. He had risked his life for people who called him a flatfoot when he wasn't protecting their worldly goods. So it was pretty hard to decide on killing a man. He decided finally because he knew it was the only way to save the only life he knew. You just don't shrug off nineteen years of your life. Nineteen tough years. It was all he had. And when you matched that up to a punk like Frankie, Frankie's life became unimportant.

He had really risked his own life for a lot of years, right? Then it seemed that one small-time punk's life wasn't much to take in payment for that service. Frankie was scheduled for an early grave anyway. That's the way he had to think. He was afraid to think about it any other way.

Hamilton sat for a long time in the dark of his living room, and watched the city's neon night reflecting in his window. Finally, he set his glass down and unlocked his desk to take out Mary Blair's diary and the small address book he'd taken from her apartment.

He returned to his chair and snapped on the reading light. Which one do I use? he thought. There isn't much choice. It has to be the address book. He could explain why he'd

179

missed it when he'd searched Frankie's room. And he could explain why Frankie had it in his room. He could speculate on that for Kinsmiller. Frankie wouldn't be around to argue. Frankie had it because he'd been in a hurry when he'd killed the girl. He would have grabbed anything that might have his name in it. That's how he'd guess at it when it turned up in his pocket.

That's how he'd tell it after he'd killed him. It was too bad that he didn't have a murder weapon to plant. Where would he get a murder weapon with two twenty-millimeter striking faces on it? Was there such a thing? He'd check that report again just to be sure. He laid the address book on the smoking stand beside the chair and picked up the diary.

And that leaves the mysterious lover and this book, he thought. The element of risk in his plan. They might not question her being pregnant. The risk, then, was in the lover walking into the police station and making a confession after he'd killed Frankie. Small risk in that . . . It was a chance he had to take.

There was no sense in taking the risk of the diary being around too. He thumbed the gold-edged pages and unconsciously stopped at the place where he'd left off before. He found himself hoping she had not named her lover as he searched for her next reference to him.

It was dated May 2.

Last night he made love to me for the first time. I think I wanted— was waiting for it to happen. It was frightening and lovely and so strange, as though I'd become another person after waiting for it to happen for so long. I talked to D. about it. I had to. I just knew there was something wrong with me to act like that. Love is strange, she told me. I think it must be normal then. I feel as though I

180

wanted it to happen, like I'd planned it. I wore the black panties and bra too. Strange and frightening. I think that I love him. I must love him to do that.

There were two empty lines under that, and then:

I'm so terribly frightened and mixed up. I'll see him again tonight.

Hamilton closed the book very firmly and finished his drink. He carried the book into the kitchen, holding the whiskey bottle under his arm, and carried them both to the sink. He took a long drink from the bottle.

He'd be goddamned if he wanted to read about her getting laid, he thought. He didn't want to know who the bastard was. He had Frankie. Hamilton stood at the sink, burning the diary in the white basin and drinking from the bottle.

The smoke had made a black smudge on the wall behind the sink when he'd finished. But by then he was too drunk to care. He did not care either that the long-awaited rain was cooling the city outside.

15

It was still raining on Monday morning when Rawls reached the parking lot behind the courthouse. The city had changed its sun-brassy dress to one of misty gray, and it wore that under clouds that seemed to touch the tops of the dark buildings.

It rained in spurts of fury, lashing the streets with pounding cloud bursts that turned the gutters into miniature rapids filled with the mad fleet of litter.

Rawls did not feel up to a quarterback dash from his car to the courthouse between spurts. He did not feel up to even a casual walk. He could possibly manage a nice easy crawl, he imagined. And the way he felt, he wasn't eager for that.

God, those bastards had worked him over good. It would be nice to imagine them as poor misguided kids, unable to understand what he was trying to do, as the book said. But it's pretty hard to do that when you have five stitches in your head and three teeth missing, and are generally sore all over. It hadn't been any picnic to get those broken teeth extracted either. Altogether, feeling as he did, he had to doubt the wisdom of trying to see his attackers as poor misguided kids.

He would honestly like to be able to smile and accept that book wisdom and forget that his mouth felt like hamburger inside, and that he looked like hell with stitches in his head

182

and half his face decorated in purple and yellow. But since he couldn't accept it in his present condition, he compromised with himself. He was going to knock Patsy square on his ass the next time he saw him, if he did. And *then* he was going to imagine him as a poor misguided kid.

And too, there was a reluctance in him to spend his day explaining how he'd come by all of his decorations. Not that he gave a damn about the way he looked. It didn't change his outlook on his parolees or anything like that. But there was something about his worked-over look that wasn't going to help his argument for Frankie. That worried him. Anyway, he was prepared to argue like hell to put his points across with Cochan. Argue? No. He wasn't going to argue, he was going to present his facts. He was right in what he'd done, and that should be enough. He could start arguing if being right wasn't enough.

Innocent until proved guilty. He'd take those four words right up to the governor if he had to. If it rocked the boat, tough. The words, as far as he was concerned, expressed a basic right of every man. And to hell with people who tried to ration them out. To hell with people who tried to change his mind on that.

He simply could not understand how else they expected him to do his job. They had told him that equal justice was something that his men were entitled to. They couldn't be serious about violating Frankie's parole after a court had freed him. Why not just leave it up to the police to violate parolees then? Why not eliminate parole agents completely, and tell a man coming out of prison not to unpack his bags, because the first time he was picked up on suspicion of anything he was going back. Why not that?

183

What the hell was his job if he couldn't assure his parolees equal justice? An equal portion of the same thing that had made them parolees in the first place.

You couldn't go around thinking that justice was a piece of luck when you received it. He had told his men that they were entitled to equal justice. Was he supposed to decide what equal meant too? It was in the book, in black and white. Frankie had got that with his help. Was he expected to tell him now that equal didn't quite mean that in his case? That it simply meant that he would have to accept less than that?

Did it? You just couldn't tell Rawls that it did.

Cochan was telling him exactly that fifteen minutes later after saying that he looked like hell. Cochan, whom he had known since he'd joined the department, and even had an occasional drink with, had also seemed to forget his first name. He was now Rawls to a man who had called him by his first name yesterday.

"I've been reading Trumper's case, Rawls," he said. "I had his records brought over here from your office. You understand why?"

Rawls nodded. "Yes. I suppose you'd be interested in knowing why—"

"Don't suppose anything, Rawls," Cochan snapped. "You should know exactly why. Do you?"

"Yes. Of course I do."

"And I can't say that I'm happy about what I've read." Cochan shoved the report aside. "I wonder what in hell you think you know about this man with the little information you have here on him. How many times have you interviewed him?"

"Six or seven times, I believe."

184

"You believe?" Cochan said. "Don't you even know how many times you've seen him?"

"Seven," Rawls said. "Six monthly visits and once at the café where he worked."

"You haven't spent much time with him then."

"Not enough." Rawls' mouth was tight. "I have a hundred and some cases besides—"

"I'm aware of how many cases you have."

"—his that I see every month," Rawls finished.

"Have you or haven't you spent a lot of time with this man's case?"

"Oh, wait a minute now," Rawls said. "I know what you're getting at. And we can stop it right here."

"What am I getting at?" Cochan shouted. "Isn't it what you suppose I'm getting at? Isn't it what you think I'm getting at, but don't know? That's what you're doing with Trumper—you *think* he's innocent."

"You're trying to establish that I don't know enough about the man's case," Rawls said angrily. "You're trying to prove that I don't know enough about the man to make the decisions that I made. That's what this is all about, isn't it?"

"That's exactly what this is all about. Seven hours in six months. How in hell can you think you know this man well enough to do what you did?"

"And just who around here has spent more time with him to say that I'm wrong?" Rawls shouted. "You? Do you have a day-by-day six-month report on Trumper from someone else around here that makes you an authority? I've got seven hours to back my decision. How much time with him have you got? You didn't even know his name until it hit your desk on a police report."

185

"You don't have to shout."

"To hell I don't," Rawls said. "If I don't start making loud noises right now, I'm going to wind up stamping a violated tag on Trumper's file, because I've let someone talk me into believing that I can't be sure about the man. I'm making loud noises because I know more about Frankie Trumper than I do about any of my cases. Not much more, but that isn't the question in his case."

"What exactly is the question then?" Cochan asked quietly.

"The question is, if this department is going to be pressured into violating a man's parole by public opinion and a DA's feelings."

"I think the question is what protection we can offer society," Cochan said. "That's our first function, protecting society."

"Frankie Trumper is a part of society," Rawls said. "Do we protect it all or just part of it?"

"I know this. . . ."

"He has been cleared of the crime and ordered free by the court."

"Technically."

"Is there another place he has to clear himself? I would like to know that."

They stared at each other in silence. "Well," Cochan said, picking up Trumper's file. "Let's consider our debt to society greater than it is to any single individual."

"Society *is* individuals."

Cochan fingered the file and stared at Rawls coldly. "Sometimes it's up to us to make the right choice. We try to

186

make the choice in favor of society as a whole. We're not blessed with the insight of gods. At least I'm not. Laws are made to protect the people; sometimes they need some common sense to back them up."

"This isn't the same thing," Rawls said. "It just isn't the same thing."

Cochan extended the file over the desk. "Think about it, will you, Chuck?"

Oh, so it's Chuck now, Rawls thought.

"Think about it and let me know what you decide."

Rawls took the file and looked squarely at Cochan. "I'll think about it, Mr. Cochan," he said deliberately. "But I can tell you right now that you can call the commissioner, and the DA, and you can tell them that seven hours makes me the authority on Trumper. I'm not going to violate him. And, what's more, if someone else does I'm going as high as I can with the question of where *he* got his authority. I've got to sign that violation to make it legal. That's my job."

"The aftereffects of your decision are yours too," Cochan said. "Think of that. Don't be hasty with this, Chuck. It could ruin your career if you're wrong. If this man, freed by a technicality and by your stubbornness, commits a crime next week, or next year, whenever he does it's going to fall right on you, and as a civil servant you wouldn't be able to get a job sweeping streets in this city. The wrong decision is the one that they'll look at on your record. It might ruin you, Chuck."

"It could ruin a man's life too," Rawls said simply. "One that I've been helping him build." He walked to the door and paused, undecided for a moment. Then he shrugged and went out. Cochan hadn't mentioned his face again, he remembered.

187

Maybe it was an everyday happening around here. It could be that he was the one who didn't understand. It could be that he was actually wrong when it was too late to be wrong.

He tried not to think about that as he walked down the long corridor and into his office. You were only wrong like that once.

He hoped he wasn't.

Hamilton sat at his desk in the squad room and remembered the words that the booking sergeant had written below Frankie's name on the booking sheet. "Suspect released from custody 09:15 A.M., 18th September, 1967, by authority of attached court order."

They let him go, Hamilton thought.

And he had watched him go as he cleared his desk, knowing that they were letting a dead man walk out. He had not felt the smallest urge to stop him. He couldn't change his plans now. It was nineteen years, a court order, and a suspension too late for a change of plans. This morning he had cleaned his service revolver and experienced the feeling of preparing to kill a man. Still, being prepared to do that had been his job every day of his adult life, if you wanted to look at it like that.

He wanted to look at it like that. But this time he knew in advance which life he would take. That was the only difference. You couldn't blame him because things had worked out wrong. He was a good cop. He'd always been a good cop. He had the right to protect his own life, didn't he? What was the sense of being a cop if you couldn't protect everything you had worked for all your life?

Trumper was only a punk. There were a million punks in the city and he could tell you all about punks. One less would

188

be a blessing, a sort of "keep the city free of punks" program. You couldn't argue about the advantages in that.

Not when it seemed too late to change your mind.

Hamilton glanced at his watch. It was nine-twenty. His suspension would be effective at ten. It didn't matter. It would take Frankie only twenty minutes to reach his room by bus. He would wait fifteen minutes more, he decided.

He stared at the neatly stacked papers on his desk. A pile of shit, he decided. That's what was at the end of his being a cop. A pile of shit that didn't belong on his desk. And another paper suspending him because he hadn't shoveled it properly. That's what they'd give him if he let them.

He looked at his watch again and up at the windows. The rain seemed to make the station house a comfortable place, shutting off the city with a watery curtain. He had always liked the rain. He pulled the case file across his desk and began to read the parts that wouldn't fit so well when he solved it with his .38. He didn't like that autopsy, and wished fervently that Mary Blair had not been pregnant. It would be hard to explain that. It would be hard to explain that murder weapon too.

Whatever he said it was wouldn't be contradicted by Frankie.

At nine-thirty the turnkey from the cell block upstairs came into the room and walked over to his desk. The turnkey did not particularly like Hamilton. He had often wished that the bastard would someday do something that would get him busted off the force. And now that it appeared that he had, the turnkey couldn't resist twisting the knife a little. He lit a cigarette casually and smiled.

"Your friend left you a present upstairs," he said. "A little memento for you."

189

Hamilton watched him silently as he placed Frankie's hand exerciser on the desk.

The turnkey grinned broadly. "Thought you might like it as a trophy of the one who got away."

Hamilton picked up the exerciser silently and studied it. It appeared to be no more than an oversize nutcracker with a tension spring holding the two plastic handles apart. Hamilton squeezed it, watching the turnkey. "How'd you like it shoved up your ass in memory of me?" he asked seriously.

"Tsk, tsk," the turnkey said. "No sense of humor at all. That's the trouble with you old—"

"Get the hell away from me!" Hamilton said.

"Didn't you get the word?" the turnkey asked in surprise. "You don't give orders around here." He paused and made a show of looking at his watch. "Well, well," he went on. "I seem to be wrong. That isn't effective until ten o'clock, is it? Mind if I wait around till then? I'd sure like to tell you to kiss my—"

"I said get the hell away from me!" Hamilton said. And as he said it, he half rose from his chair and slammed his fist against the desktop, forgetting that he still held the hand exerciser. He also forgot that his desktop was covered with glass. He had bought that glass himself. He had bought a good, thick piece of glass with fine wire mesh in its center so that it wouldn't be breaking when everyday items such as brass knuckles and pistols were dropped on it. He forgot that and was mildly surprised at the two things that happened when his fist hit the desk. He was surprised that the glass cracked loudly into a patch of spider-web lines. He was also surprised to notice that the turnkey was passing through the door leading to the can when he looked up from the first surprise.

190

The desk sergeant was watching him from across the room.

Hamilton ignored him and stared at the glass. Clyde, that idiot at the lab, had once told him some things about glass. He had told him things like why an ordinary type of glass will cut you all to hell if you happen to be unfortunate enough to go through it. And he had told him why glass that has been reinforced will not. Hamilton had taken Clyde's explanation to mean simply that the first type of glass broke into jagged edges, while the second type crumbled. It crumbled, and was held together by its reinforcement.

The glass on his desk had crumbled where the handles of the exerciser had struck it. There were two white circles of powdered glass surrounded by a dinner-plate-size spider web of cracks.

It was suddenly all very interesting to Hamilton. While he was not particularly interested in glass at the moment, even when it was his own desktop, and was more concerned with holes like the one he was going to put in Frankie, he was still very intrigued by these particular circles of broken glass.

He opened the file and consulted the autopsy: A hammer-type weapon, with a striking face of approximately twenty millimeters. He then debated the merit of Clyde's theory on the wounds in Mary Blair's skull being made simultaneously, and stared at Frankie's hand exerciser.

That wasn't a hammer-type object, he thought. Unless you held it and imagined your arm as the handle of the hammer. And while you were holding it, there was about an inch of both handles of this oversize nutcracker sticking out of your hand. That made *two* striking faces. Two twenty-millimeter striking faces. That made a goddamn two-headed hammer!

191

That made a murder weapon if you hit someone on the head with it, like he'd hit that desk.

He'd hit the glass pretty hard. It would take a pretty strong man to drive those handles through a person's skull.

That punk Frankie was pretty strong, he remembered. That punk also had this thing in his pocket when he'd been picked up. It followed that he was accustomed to carrying it. He was a muscle freak, wasn't he?

He consulted the autopsy some more and studied the handles of the exerciser. It was disappointing to see that he had chipped the plastic ends deeply by hitting the glass. That idiot Clyde might have been able to match that chip he'd found in Mary Blair's skull to one of the handles. He could now possibly testify to the chip being of the same type of plastic.

Hamilton was amazed. It was beginning to look like that punk really *did* do it. He could probably prove it now. He could prove it because Frankie would have some additional parts of the puzzle on him when they found him. The only thing that could clear Frankie was her being pregnant; he just couldn't risk him going free on that.

Could he?

He looked at his watch. It was nine thirty-seven. How do I play it? he thought. Do I take this to Kinsmiller? That son-of-a-bitch really did this. Do I take this in there and go through it again? There was a righteous anger growing in him. Did he let that murdering son-of-a-bitch get a chance to get away with this again? Did he let those idiots turn him loose again?

He picked up his hat and started for the door.

16

Frankie had got wet walking from the bus stop to the rooming house. It was the only time in his life that he could remember not minding getting wet.

He had beaten the rap, and there was a sudden knowledge in his mind that he had not expected to beat it. Somewhere in his mind he had seen himself walking down that long corridor with the green door at its end, and knowing that the chair was on the other side.

He had known that it was a dream, because when he went like that you could bet he'd have to be dragged every foot of the way. A lousy dream. He would have gone fighting them. And he had somehow expected it to work out that way.

He had beaten them. Rawls had helped him, all right, but it was him who called the shots. He'd made some mistakes and he'd still beaten the stupid bastards. He'd have to act grateful to Rawls, he supposed. He'd like to see the expression on the pious bastard's face if he knew how easy he'd been fooled.

But he'd never know.

Nobody would know now. He stood for a moment in the doorway to his room and smelled the damp, stale smell of sweat and old furniture that stank of himself and the room's past occupants when it was damp. The room sure was a hole.

He remembered that he had been ashamed to bring Mary Blair up there. He felt very alone. Everything had worked out all right, he thought. He should be the happiest guy alive. He should feel good. Him, Frankie, he'd beaten the rap, he was free and clear.

He sat down on his bed and stared at the rain pounding in bursts on the dirty windows. His hands shook as he lit a cigarette. There was no fear of death behind his thoughts now. He could relax and think about Mary without worrying about the chair. But he could not think about her without wondering why she had been so stupid.

Stupid. She had been lousy, stinking stupid. He had not planned to hurt her when he'd agreed to pick her up after the dance. He was only going to show her what a simple bitch she was with that love crap.

He was going to show her that love came in a package supplied by Iggy. He was tired of it anyway. She didn't even cry anymore; she'd just get one of those sad, stupid smiles on her face and agree with him.

Frankie thought about it. I mean what's the kick in banging some stupid little broad who was liking it? Like she'd let you call her a whore and agree with you. She'd say, "Yes, I'm your whore." She'd say that with a funny little catch in her voice, and then she'd say, "Because I love you."

All right. All right. So what if he'd sort of liked the way things had worked out? So what if he'd wondered what would have been said if she didn't have a dose of Spanish fly. He'd wondered once what would have happened if he'd never started giving her the stuff, and even if the stuff really worked.

He had wondered what it would be like to be loved like that. He didn't love her, because she was an uptown bitch

194

who'd never think of loving him if it wasn't for that stuff Iggy gave him.

He had to know. He was going to try, and when she said no, he was going to show her that she'd screw anybody; all it took was a dose of fly.

She had let him in through the back door after the dance and moved into his arms in the semidarkness.

"I thought you weren't coming," she said. "I thought I'd have to go home alone."

"You do."

"Why, Frankie?"

He shrugged. "Just something that came up. I have to take care of it." He slid his hands down her back and pulled her hips against him, waiting for her to recoil. "I got an hour or so though."

She moved against him, burying her face against his neck. "That's a lot of time." Her lips were very warm on his face and he could smell the mintlike freshness of her. "Do you want to make love?" she asked.

That's not what you're supposed to say, Frankie thought. You're not supposed to want to, unless . . . unless . . . He kissed her, letting his hand find the zipper of her skirt.

"Wait," she said, moving away.

Now she'll say it, he thought. Get your hands off me, you cheap pig. Go ahead, say it.

She took his hand. "The locker room," she said. "There are some exercise mats there. Does that give you any ideas?"

It gave Frankie ideas. He couldn't understand it. She had undressed slowly and unembarrassedly in the locker room, piling her clothes in a neat stack. He realized that she was very beautiful. Why was she doing this? He hadn't given her anything to give her hot pants.

Why?

She joined him on the mat, pressing her now familiar warmth against him. Maybe she did . . . but he didn't believe in that. But maybe she . . .

"You've got more than ideas," she said. "So have I."

And that would have been all right if it had ended there, Frankie knew. But she had to make a fool out of him. He knew that there had to be some reason that she was so willing.

They lay together, tired and content. "You've never said it," she whispered.

"What?"

She was silent.

He held her and realized what she wanted to hear him say. He had never told anybody that, he didn't know how to say it. It was very difficult to hold her and say, "I love you."

"Yes," she sighed. "I'm glad because that makes things all right."

He had no idea what it made all right. He did not really care until he found out while he was dressing.

She remained on the mat, resting with her hands folded on her stomach. And she smiled contentedly at him when he'd held up her clothes.

"We're going to have a baby, Frankie," she said softly, and smiled.

She should not have told him.

Because he knew then what a fool she had made out of him. He knew that there had to be some reason for her letting him make love to her without that junk. And there it was! The bitch was pregnant. That was the only reason she'd let him!

He did not remember hitting her. He had hit her with the hand exerciser but he could not remember taking it from his

196

pocket. He had jerked her to her feet, ready to tell her what a pig she was. But he had hit her instead, and she had lain on the tile floor, with blood under her head.

He had sat there and watched her for a long time before he figured out what to do. He had wrapped her head in a towel and pulled her blouse and skirt back on her. He put her underclothes in his pocket because they were too much trouble. Then he had cleaned the tile floor and found her purse before he'd carried her down the alley until he could no longer carry her, and he had dragged her a way after that, before he'd left her behind the bar.

He had been very careful even then, Frankie thought. He had burned her underclothes and the towel, and wiped the purse carefully with a handkerchief after he'd taken the key out.

There was only that key, he remembered. He'd kept that key.

He rose from the bed and opened the door to the closet. The key was still where he'd left it. He burned the red tag in his ashtray, and pushed the key through a crack under the windowsill and listened to it fall down between the walls.

He was safe.

He went back to the bed. No, not quite, he remembered. He took the package Iggy had sold him and dumped the powder out the window into the rain.

He should really save some of it, he thought. He should use some of it on that bitch across the hall. Well, he could get some more later, he decided. He had better not fool with her for a while. He'd better just take it easy.

He closed the window and burned the empty package in the ashtray before returning to the bed. Now he was safe. He would take it easy for a while. But that one across the hall was next. He wondered how he could get into her pants without raping her.

She was a tramp anyway. He'd stick to tramps from now on. He didn't want to get involved with a murder again. All he wanted to do was love them. He'd told Mary he loved her, hadn't he?

He sat with his head in his hands. He would be very careful the next time, even if he had beaten the rap. He felt a sudden sadness about Mary.

Hamilton parked his car in front of the apartment house and stared at the rain sweeping the street. The wind was cold, like the coldness inside him. It was something he really didn't want to do. It was one of those things that came up and you wished that it hadn't. But there was nothing he could do about it. He couldn't take Frankie into court and have everything come out. They would wonder why he hadn't investigated what Dian Kenton had told him about Mary's lover.

What could he say then? He didn't need to? He was framing Frankie? He just couldn't risk a big court trial now, even if he knew that the punk was guilty. It had to be here, and now, where only certain evidence was brought up.

You could never trust a punk.

He wondered how Frankie had managed to kill her. Where had he run across her? He wished he hadn't burned that diary now. There were some questions that he wanted answered for himself.

But they wouldn't be answered now, they couldn't be.

That murdering son-of-a-bitch had killed her. What the hell did it matter how or why?

198

This would be the end of it, he thought. And then he knew that it wouldn't be. He would always be waiting for that nameless lover to show up and bring out all of the points of his affair with the girl. And they would know then that he had tried to hide these points. And being a cop, he knew that cops would wonder about that, and check on it. And it might all come out then. They would smell a frame no matter how guilty Frankie was. He would have to worry about it the rest of his life. Like a lousy punk.

Well?

He got out of the car and felt the lash of the rain strike his face. He walked slowly to the building and started up the stairs with a heavy step.

He opened his jacket and pulled his service revolver when he reached 3-C. He knocked and placed his left hand flat against the door, waiting until he saw it begin to open before he shoved violently and felt it slam into Frankie, sending him back off balance as he crouched into the room.

"What the hell—" Frankie stopped, seeing the gun.

"Don't blink, punk," Hamilton said. "Get up against the wall, you know the position. Make one screwy move and you're dead."

Frankie stared at him.

"Get up against that wall, you son-of-a-bitch."

Hamilton searched him. Then picked up his jacket from the back of the chair and watched Frankie's back as he shoved Mary Blair's address book into the inside pocket.

"You learn slow, don't you, cop?" Frankie asked. "I'm free, you know. I don't even think you're still on the force."

Hamilton stood silently behind him for a long while before he said, "Why'd you kill her, Frankie?"

Frankie said nothing.

"With that hand exerciser of yours, Frankie," Hamilton said, and watched him stiffen. "That was pretty cute. You had the murder weapon right on you all the time. You even had the lieutenant send it to you in your cell. Who'd think of looking for a murder weapon in the police station, huh?"

"You got nothing on me, cop," Frankie said. "I don't know what you're running your mouth about."

"Did you see her first in the hash house or when you delivered coffee? I know all about that too."

"You can't prove a thing," Frankie said. "The court sprung me, remember? There ain't any way you can pin it on me."

"We'll get a new indictment," Hamilton assured him. "Go ahead, be a jailhouse lawyer, see what it gets you. Call your big-shot friend, Rawls, and see what that gets you. You're not beating this one."

"I'll beat it."

Hamilton walked close behind him and pressed the nose of the .38 behind his ear. "How'd you do it, punk? Did you grab her like some animal and drag her into that alley? You're a pig, Frankie, a filthy slimy pig. That's the only way your kind can get a woman, isn't it?"

Frankie was silent and Hamilton watched the sweat creeping down the back of his neck. "We got all we need this time, Frankie," he added. "The body, the murder weapon, witnesses that saw you talking to her, and we got you."

"It ain't enough," Frankie whispered.

"Believe me, it's enough to convict an animal like you. Did she spit in your face while you were doing it? She must have felt like a slimy snake was on her." He paused and leaned

200

close. "How about it, Frankie?" he shouted. "A pig like you . . ."

Frankie took his arms down from the wall. "Wait," he said.

"Stand still, you bastard," Hamilton hissed. "You raped her, didn't you? Because she wouldn't let a thing like you near her."

"Wait," Frankie said again, turning around to look at Hamilton. "You lousy bastard," he said simply, and began to cry silently.

Hamilton backed up. "Get your jacket, punk," he said.

The hall was empty when they went out of the room.

"We'll use the back steps," Hamilton said.

Frankie said nothing. He turned down the hall, wishing he could stop crying because he didn't want them to know that he was crying for her.

And he didn't want to die. The hall reminded him of the long, polished hall in the death house where there was that green door at the end. He wondered briefly if Rawls would help him again . . . if . . .

He wondered suddenly where Hamilton was, realizing that he was not handcuffed. He was not being held by the arm. He had started to turn around when the slug smashed through his spine and clipped off the top of his heart before tearing a cup-size hole in his upper chest on its way out.

Frankie never heard the shot. He thought in that last instant of Mary Blair. And then he twitched slightly and died.

Hamilton checked to assure himself that Frankie was dead before he went down to the second floor to the telephone there. He was already beginning to wonder if he'd made any mistakes as he dialed the number of the station house.

17

September 22 was a Friday.

Tomorrow would be the first day of autumn. The city had been suddenly wrapped in the colorful skirts of a frost-touched fall. The day was cool and crisp with a smoky blue sky.

But Rawls was not interested in summer's sudden death. Neither was he interested in the fact that this Friday did not seem to be meeting the standards of past Fridays.

It was turning out to be not too bad a day, after a week of gloomy anticipation, of waiting for the ax to fall. He had waited for its fall since Frankie Trumper had died while trying to escape arrest.

He imagined that he felt something like a condemned man must feel when the jury is out, waiting for the retribution that would be ordered for his mistakes. As the public defender had recommended to him, he would settle for mercy rather than justice for his mistakes.

He had been wrong about Frankie. The grand jury had met, examined the facts, and quietly closed the books on Frankie Trumper with the view that justice had been served to all concerned. You couldn't argue with the grand jury.

Rawls had waited for his own serving of justice for the

rest of the week. He was a bit resentful about the slowness of it. He now agreed that he had been a fool, he had very nearly become an obstruction to justice with his by-the-book stubbornness.

It was a bit confusing; somehow he could still see flaws in the whole thing. But matters were no longer simply black and white. He had seen the light when the grand jury had ruled that no further investigation was needed into the matter of Frankie Trumper.

Rawls had been ready all week to admit that he had been wrong. He would never again let noble thoughts stand in the way of a working system and make a damn fool out of him.

He was ready to admit it, and he wished like hell that Cochan or the commissioner would go ahead and drop that ax they were holding over his head so he could see what the price had been for stupid ideals. He'd like to learn the consequences of letting some lousy punk make a fool out of him. He felt very put upon.

The price, as it turned out, when it was delivered by Cochan at ten o'clock Friday morning was puzzling. He would be neither fired nor transferred for his mistaken faith in Frankie. He had been lucky, Cochan said. They had considered his inexperience, and though his devotion to doing his job was perhaps a bit overzealous, faith in men was hard to find.

They would appreciate it if he wasn't quite so devoted in that way in the future.

He sat at his desk then and felt cheated. He had expected something to happen; perhaps he had expected to become a sacrifice to the system. And he wondered if there was a system, or if there was no more than men, doing jobs the best way they could.

He looked at the plaque on his door and remembered that Friday was a special day for Frankie too.

They were burying him today, at eleven.

He shrugged and turned to the work on his desk. He paused. In a sense, he owed Frankie something. He would no longer have any faith in a punk. He could thank Frankie for that.

But he couldn't think like that, could he? he asked himself. For some reason he felt a disappointment in the thought. He had sold himself rather cheaply, hadn't he? He had sold his faith in men and those basic rights pretty easily when everything that had happened had not changed the meaning behind those rights a bit.

He sat at the desk, and thought about it for a long time, feeling the sun warm on his back. Those rights still belonged to everybody, he thought. He decided that he did owe Frankie something.

He was the only one at the funeral.